"KATRINA, LAST NIGHT HAPPENED BECAUSE YOU WANTED ME AND I WANTED YOU," MIKE INSISTED ANGRILY.

"How could I want you when I totally loathe you?" Katrina cried, tears welling in her eyes.

"You are a coward, and the worst liar I've ever known, because you're even willing to lie to yourself."

"The only liar around here is you! You told me to trust you, and you're nothing but a sham—just like last night, just like everything that goes on between us."

Suddenly he grabbed her and kissed her hungrily; then he let her go, leaving her trembling, breathless. "Now do you want to tell me that last night was a sham?"

CANDLELIGHT ECSTASY CLASSIC ROMANCES

THE GAME IS PLAYED,
Amii Lorin
TENDER YEARNINGS,
Elaine Raco Chase
WAGERED WEEKEND,
Jayne Castle
LOVE'S ENCORE,
Rachel Ryan

CANDLELIGHT ECSTASY ROMANCES®

468 NO WAY TO TREAT A LADY, *Jane Atkin*
469 PASSION AND POSSESSION, *Kathy Clark*
470 WILD TEMPTATION, *Helen Conrad*
471 KING OF SEDUCTION, *Alison Tyler*
472 TRIPLE THREAT, *Eleanor Woods*
473 SWEET TEMPEST, *Eileen Bryan*

EDEN'S SPELL

Heather Graham

A CANDLELIGHT ECSTASY ROMANCE®

Published by
Dell Publishing Co., Inc.
1 Dag Hammarskjold Plaza
New York, New York 10017

In loving memory of Ellsworth D. "Dan" Graham,
my favorite Navy man World War II

ISBN: 0-440-12224-4

Printed in the United States of America

December 1986

10 9 8 7 6 5 4 3 2 1

WFH

To Our Readers:

We have been delighted with your enthusiastic response to Candlelight Ecstasy Romances®, and we thank you for the interest you have shown in this exciting series.

In the upcoming months we will continue to present the distinctive sensuous love stories you have come to expect only from Ecstasy. We look forward to bringing you many more books from your favorite authors and also the very finest work from new authors of contemporary romantic fiction.

As always, we are striving to present the unique, absorbing love stories that you enjoy most—books that are more than ordinary romance. Your suggestions and comments are always welcome. Please write to us at the address below.

Sincerely,

The Editors
Candlelight Romances
1 Dag Hammarskjold Plaza
New York, New York 10017

EDEN'S SPELL

PROLOGUE

"Mom! Mom! Come quick!"

Katrina started slightly. Normally, she would have been attuned to the urgency in Jason's voice and responded instantly to his call.

But today . . .

Something about today had cast her so deeply into her own thoughts that she remained where she was, cocooned in a dream world.

It might have been the wind; it might have been the lulling dip of the palm fronds, or the slow ripples moving across the surface of the pond. There was a scent of wild orchids in the air today, too, and it might have been that scent that had reminded her so much of James. Or maybe it was just the way she was lying, stretched over the cool sand, the way they had so often done together.

"This is it, Katrina! The closest thing to Eden this side of heaven! Our Eden, our paradise!"

James seemed to have materialized before her, tall, slender, very, very tan, his dark hair streaked platinum by the sun. His grin, boyish and mischievous, lit up his face, and his arms embraced the air with enthusiasm.

And she laughed happily.

He slid down beside her, idly running his fingers along her bare ribs. "Just like Eve!" He teased her, his sandy eyes twinkling. "Pure trouble, pure temptation!"

"Trouble! I resent that. And I can't possibly be temptation! There isn't an apple tree anywhere on this island!"

Impatiently he tugged at the tie to her bikini top, frowning as the knot refused to give. "Sea grapes," he told her absently. "We have sea grapes."

"Ugh!" Katrina muttered, smiling at his frustrated attempts to sweep away her top. In a minute, of course, he would give up, asking her if she hadn't been in the Navy at some point in life, learning to make foolproof knots. Then she would protest demurely that they were in the open, and he would remind her that it was their island, and she would strip away the top with wanton dexterity. But for now . . .

"I can't imagine tempting anyone with sea grapes," she said sweetly, her voice catching slightly as he continued to tug away.

"Forget about sea grapes and apples, my love. You're temptation enough without them." And then he bent over her and cradled her head between his palms, tenderly, sensually massaging her cheeks with his thumbs as his eyes searched hers. His voice had lost its teasing quality. "I'm the luckiest man in the universe. . . ."

His lips touched hers, then moved to her throat, and she felt the delicious rush of desire sweep through her that never failed when they touched. "And the sexiest . . ." she whispered back to him, digging her fingers into his hair as he lightly bit her nipple through the fabric. "And the most—"

"Mom!"

This time Jason's shriek did penetrate the fog of her thoughts. Suddenly panicked at the sound of his voice, she catapulted to her feet, spinning like a dancer on her bare toes for a moment as she desperately tried to locate his position.

"Jason! Where are you?"

There was no answer.

"Jason!"

Still no answer.

The island was only two miles long and a mile wide, but at the moment it seemed much bigger. Katrina began to wonder feverishly what could possibly have happened to make Jason cry out so.

She was already running. Sea grapes and palms ripped at her hair as she tore through the foliage, and straggling mangrove roots threatened to trip her, but this was her island, and she was accustomed to its terrain.

South . . . she was certain that the cry had come from the south. She passed the second brackish inland pool, which was almost dry with the lack of rain.

"Jason!"

She screamed her son's name out again. And again, there was no answer. Thoughts tumbled wildly through her mind. She shouldn't have stayed on here. She'd survived nicely for the last five years, yes, but if something had happened to her son, happened because they lived alone in a subtropical jungle, she would never forgive herself.

Forgive herself! She wouldn't want to go on living! Not if she lost Jason too. . . .

He was all right, she tried to console herself. He could swim like a fish, and he had the sense not to go in the water alone, anyway. He climbed trees, yes, but none of the trees on the island was very high. As for snakes, he knew which were harmless, and so far, they'd never seen a moccasin, or a coral snake.

She kept running, led by instinct. Past a patch of crotons, wild hibiscus, and bitter cherry, she found the path, which was shaded by a line of palm trees. It was almost dusk, and the sun was casting patterns of red and orange and primitive pink.

The pool was before her. She was in the dark, cool shade of the palm trees, but it was in light: A mist of pure gold light.

"Jason!" Katrina shouted, and then fell dead silent.

She was shocked into stillness by the sight that greeted her. It was a man, she was certain. Or almost certain. He was standing at the far side of the pool, beneath the magic spectrum of sunlight. He was helmeted and uniformed, as if he had prepared for a walk in space. His uniform was silver, catching the sun's rays, giving off a glowing aura.

All that was actually visible of him were his eyes. And like his uniform they seemed to be silver. Shimmering, penetrating silver.

Yet more important than his appearance—far more important!—was the fact that he was holding Jason in his silver-coated arms. Held with what appeared to be care, yet held because he was quite obviously unconscious—or dead.

"No!" Katrina shrieked, no longer held immobile by the incredible sight. She ran through the pool, heedless of the murky water, of the branches and roots that lay beneath, of anything. But the pool suddenly seemed so large. She was running, but her movement seemed ridiculously slow. And there was a strange ground fog.

The fog! That was it! The fog was thick and heavy and pinkish. That was what was keeping her from reaching Jason, from wrenching him from the arms of the alien and making sure that he was fine.

"My son!" she choked out hysterically. She was going to fall; she was losing her grip on consciousness. But she couldn't, not until she reached Jason.

"He'll be all right!" A gruff voice assured her, a voice filled with impatience and aggravation. Silver eyes glared at her piercingly through the glass of the helmet.

Katrina staggered and fell into the pool. Tears of frustration and fear filled her eyes. She had to get to her feet. Some insane alien spaceman was holding her son and she had to reach him.

She struggled back up, drenched. Water dripped from her hair, from her flesh, from the tight-fitting material of her strapless teal maillot. The pink fog was all around her.

She thought she heard the soft tread of footsteps; she tried to follow the sound, but it seemed to echo and reverberate and come from all around her. Her legs were too weak to hold her, and she started falling again, falling until she sat upon her knees in the water, desperately fighting the fog that embraced her body and mind.

"Jason!" she cried, her fear feeding her anger. "Give me my son!" she shouted. "Give me my son!"

Footsteps came, sloshing through the knee-high water. Katrina instinctively cringed. He was there, standing before her. Dazed, she followed his silver-clad legs way, way up to his steel-silver eyes. He was very tall, she realized. No costume could provide such an illusion of height.

"Who are you?" she screamed. He was reaching for her, and she was terrified. She scrambled to back away, but her muscles would give her no assistance. Her voice rose in its fevered pitch. "Give me my son and—"

His hands—silver gloved—fell on her shoulders. She tried to hit him, she tried to fight, but she had no strength. Despite her screams and flailing, he drew her up. Silver arms wrapped around her, and she was being carried, just as Jason had been.

"No! Let me—"

"What in *hell* are you doing here?" he demanded curtly. "You agreed to leave!"

Something he said touched her memory; but what? No. This was a dream, a foggy, misty dream. Why couldn't she remember?

Yet he was real. She tried to twist in his arms, but they were as strong as the steel of his eyes.

"This is my island! My property! What the hell are you—oh, it doesn't even matter! Just give me my son, and get off!"

"Shut up, will you? You swore not to be here! Damned woman—stubborn witch!"

Katrina couldn't believe it. He was trespassing on her property, dressed in a spacesuit, and he had the nerve—the gall!—to call her names!

"I'll throttle you! I'll see you behind bars for the rest of your life! Oh, God, where in the hell did you escape from? If my son is—hurt—in any way . . ." It was getting harder and harder to talk. The pink fog surrounding her was becoming thicker. So thick. She couldn't move; she couldn't even twist anymore. And now her mind, too, seemed to be filling with the pink fog. She could barely think; she could hardly make out her thoughts.

And he just kept carrying her, holding her tightly in his silver arms.

"I'm going to scream. Help will come; they'll cart you away!"

"Oh, dear Lord, what did I do to deserve this?"

His steel-and-silver eyes rolled toward heaven—it was a sincere plea to the Supreme Being. Then those eyes fell on her again, and she knew he was thinking once more that she was a stubborn witch.

Then there was a glint in those eyes, slightly mischievous. "You'll be out like a light soon, thank God," he muttered. "Lord, what a shrew!"

"Shrew!"

"Shrew!" he repeated.

She wanted to say more. She wanted to fight him; she wanted to scratch him bloody right through his silver suit.

But her hands wouldn't move. Nor would her lips form words. Pink enveloped everything. She felt very light. Weightless. Even ridiculously glad of the arms that touched her.

Arms . . . hands that touched her naked flesh. They were warm against the breeze, against the coming dusk. She wore nothing but the skimpy maillot with the high-cut legs, and his fingers were brushing her there, and it suddenly seemed all right. In the world of swirling pink and misty gray, it felt perfectly all right for him to be holding her, touching her so intimately.

She opened her eyes. For a moment they fastened on his. And she smiled, because he was so cute and silly in his space suit. She liked him. And he had such nice, nice eyes. Fascinating. Steel and silver, like his touch.

And steel and silver were taking over from the pink. The world grew darker. Smiling was so easy, so effortless. She didn't want to fight. She wanted to give into the darkness, to be held, to be comforted.

To be loved. . . .

It was her last thought as the pink gave way completely to steel-gray and silver. And then blackness.

CHAPTER ONE

Well, this was one fine hell of a mess, Mike Taylor decided in total frustration as he stared helplessly from the boy he had placed on the ground to the woman he carried in his arms. He was ready to kill someone—or at least shake someone senseless.

The island was supposed to have been evacuated for his top-secret, classified project, and instead he had unwittingly received two human guinea pigs!

He sighed, then realized with disgust that the woman had managed to dislodge his helmet—and therefore his breathing apparatus. He'd better start moving; he could already detect the sweet smell of 44DFS seeping into his air supply.

She was in his arms; might as well take her first.

Clumsy in his heavy suit, Mike moved carefully through the remaining mangrove terrain of the south side of the island. His dinghy had been pulled onto the only bare ten feet of beach he had been able to find. He carefully set her into it, resting her head against one of the orange Navy-ration life-preservers. With both annoyance and curiosity, he found himself staring at her.

She was a tiny creature; no more than five two, and maybe a hundred pounds. Her hair was very long and wild and wet as it lay plastered against her bare back. Even wet, though, it gleamed with an undeniable sheen of red. Probably a deep dark red, an auburn. Yes, it had been auburn, shining in the sun like a burst of glory in those first few seconds before she had stumbled into the pool. . . .

A redhead. Oh hell, it was definitely true that redheads had horrendous tempers! As if matters weren't bad enough!

But for a moment, Mike forgot the seriousness of the situation. He smiled a little, recalling again the moment he had first seen her. Her eyes had blazed in the sun. Torquoise eyes, as blue and as green as a changing sea, as crystal clear as the water that moved gently over the reefs.

And as fury laden as a cyclone.

Mike shrugged with irritation. Damn it all! Who in God's name had flubbed up so badly? They had gone through the proper procedure, obtained all the forms. . . .

The boy, Mike reminded himself. The sooner he went back for the boy, the sooner he could reach the *Maggie Mae,* and the sooner he could straighten out this mess!

But he paused again, watching her, reflecting that he had been almost as shocked as she at their confrontation. He'd expected nothing but flora and fauna; but there had been the boy, and then, her. For a second—just a split second—he'd wondered if he hadn't stumbled into some modern-day Eden. She had just appeared, half naked, that wild hair streaming over the top of her blue bathing suit so that it had seemed as though she was wearing nothing at all. A spitfire of fury and energy, beautiful and pagan, pitching into battle unarmed.

He turned away from her, irritated all over again. For God's sake! She had a son; she'd signed the damn papers. She should have been responsible and careful enough to get off the island.

Mike clumped back through the mangrove roots, unable to shake his aggravation. Logically, it was ridiculous to be so angry at her. It had been someone else's responsibility to make sure the island was cleared of civilians. There had just been something about her. . . .

Small, petite, and fragile. She had reminded him of Margo.

Mike reached the boy, and bent carefully to cradle him into his arms. He smiled then, glancing down at the sleeping form. Nice kid. He'd shown absolute fascination when he'd first discovered Mike—and Mike had discovered him. After he'd stopped screaming for his mother, he'd become very conversational.

"Oh, boy! A spaceman! Are you from Mars?"

"No. Sorry, kid." He'd had to grin. "Originally, I'm from northern Michigan. Of course, there are people who might consider that like being from Mars."

"Are you a madman?" the boy asked quite bluntly.

And Mike had laughed, then grown very somber, reminding himself that there had been one hell of a screw-up.

"No, son, I'm with the Navy. And I need you to listen, because this is very important. I need you to come to me, very slowly, very carefully, because you're going to start to fall asleep in a matter of moments. The air will appear to be pink. . . ."

Ah, yes, pink air. And thanks to the boy's feisty mother, Mike had breathed some of that pink air himself! He'd better get a move on. He didn't want to pass out himself, especially not with the three of them adrift in a little dinghy.

Mike hurried back to the tiny strip of beach. The woman was still sleeping in the dinghy, as sweetly as a little lamb. Her lips were curved into a tender smile, as if she dreamed sweet things.

Mike placed the boy against a life preserver with gentle care, then pushed the small boat away from the beach. Out in the water, he started the motor, and turned the tiller toward the *Maggie Mae.*

Away from the island, he stripped away his helmet and mask, and deeply inhaled the fresh sea air. It was good: salty, clean, and fragrant.

And yet he knew he had also inhaled something of his own invention. He had to keep blinking to see clearly, and it felt as if a soft pink blanket were closing in around him. He had to hurry.

In front of the *Maggie Mae* he cut the motor and drifted to the stern of the yacht. He caught the towline and stood, balancing carefully. He had to strip away the rest of his quarantine outfit while in the dinghy; he'd never get up the rope ladder with his two casualties in such gear.

Casualties! Dammit, there shouldn't have been any casualties!

He grunted out an unintelligible oath, dropped the silver cloth, and hefted the boy over his shoulders. Once on deck Mike hesitated, then brought the boy to the aft cabin. He laid him down upon the bunk and quickly checked his pulse, respiration, and pupils.

He was sleeping, soundly, nicely. His pulse was as strong as a young bull's. Mike pulled the covers over the boy, left him, and returned to the dinghy for the woman.

It was almost dark now. Only a few pale streaks of red and gold still touched the sky. The breeze had picked up; it had started to dry her hair, and sent it billowing in gentle velvet fans of pure copper. Mike lifted her into his arms. Her soft hair blew and wafted around his bare shoulders like a caress of silk.

Her eyes opened while he struggled up the ladder. They were brilliant with the sea's color, fascinated, fascinating.

"Hi," she murmured sweetly.

"Hi, yourself," he replied briefly.

She yawned and stretched backward; Mike teetered precariously on the ladder.

"Hey! Hold on to me!" he commanded curtly.

She giggled, and wrapped her arms tightly around his neck. Mike gasped; she was cutting his windpipe.

"Not—so—tightly!"

She just giggled. He grit his teeth. 44DFS was his baby; he should know the side effects if anyone should.

Still gasping, he hauled them both over the side of the *Maggie Mae,* and better situated his arms around her before starting for the forward cabin.

"You're cute," she told him, drawing her fingers down his cheek, seductively grazing his flesh with the tip of her nails.

"Thanks," he muttered dryly. While he was looking at her, he slammed his head against the cabin door frame when he should have ducked beneath it.

"Ouch!" she murmured, snuggling closer.

Mike paused and inhaled deeply. Her body was very warm against his naked chest; her toes were dangling against his thighs. Her breasts, high and firm against the low edge of the bathing suit, were excruciatingly feminine. She might have only been about one hundred pounds, but damn, were those pounds disposed to the right places!

He groaned slightly, and wondered for the thousandth time just who in hell had flubbed up so badly.

"Ohhh . . . you'd be much, much cuter if you'd quit scowling!" she pouted, drawing a finger over his lip.

"Quit that!" Damned side effects! But that was what it was all about: studying the side effects of 44DFS, eliminating them. As a scientist, it was so important. But as a man, he was growing concerned that he wouldn't last another minute, much less the whole night.

But 44DFS had been the driving factor in his life for over a decade now. Over a decade. Ever since Margo . . .

Mike hurried her past the roomy galley, by the dining table and the makeshift lab, and into the master's cabin. Why the hell didn't she just pass out cold, like the boy?

He knew the answer, of course. She had not received a direct shot of the stuff, as the boy had. The pellet had barely dispersed before the boy had appeared; it had received enough time to dilute before she had raced upon the scene.

And that's why she was still clinging to him, her arms wrapped around him, her huge torquoise eyes wide on him.

"You're very, very tired," he told her.

Her eyes widened still further. "Oh, no, I'm not!" she protested dreamily.

"Dammit! You've had a good whiff of 44DFS, and that means you are totally agreeable and cannot argue with me!"

Her fingers roamed through his tawny hair, ruffling it at the forehead. "I certainly don't want to argue with you!"

"Good. I'm putting you to bed. In twenty-four hours, you'll be ready to hang me again."

He laid her down upon the bunk, hoping he wasn't going to give her pneumonia by leaving her in her wet suit.

"Aren't you coming with me?" she queried.

He stared down at her, at the long red waves of hair splaying in a delicate web over the pillow, at the smooth line of her throat and the entrancing pools of her eyes.

He ground his teeth together; a hot shudder ripped through his body, and he was painfully aware that beneath his shorts his body was rigidly willing to comply with her request.

He'd had a few whiffs of the stuff himself—not that he would have needed it with such an invitation. He swore softly, pulling the covers high over her slender form.

She was his victim, and remembering her threats, he was convinced that she would never believe that he hadn't been the one to involve her in the mix-up on the island. He was going to have a lawsuit on his hands. Not him maybe, but the U.S. government and the Navy.

But it would be his work exposed to public scrutiny and criticism, long before it could be perfected. And all because some jerk hadn't done his job properly!

"Go to sleep," he told her.

She smiled. A beautiful, sweet, and inadvertently sultry smile. Mike turned to leave her, swearing again.

He hurried back to the galley, and the chart table that flanked the sink and dryer. He was growing dizzier, and very, very tired. All he wanted to do was reach command, then take a cold, cold shower and sleep off the effects of his own drug. A nap should do it. Damn it all to hell! He'd sure need the sleep; by tomorrow night at the latest he'd be dealing with a rightiously furious civilian.

Mike tapped into the radio.

"Go tell it to the Marines!" he muttered aloud, frowning then as he received nothing but static on his radio.

And that was another thing; damn the bureaucracy and red tape! This should have been left as a strictly naval venture! His liaisons should have been men he knew and trusted.

"Come in, 44DFS."

He decided to cut the military crap right to the line. "I want to know who blew this thing!"

Static answered him; then, "I don't read you, 44DFS."

"Uninhabited island, eh? I've a woman and child on board."

"That's impossible, sir. We've the consent forms right here—"

"And I've got two victims right here!" Mike interrupted in a rage. "Give me the admiral—now!"

To his credit, Admiral Larson came directly to the radio. Mike realized later that he was an okay guy to sit there and take abuse as long as he did, then, to speak soothingly without drawing rank.

"As you know, Taylor, we can't approach the vessel tonight. We'll be there by eighteen hundred tomorrow. A woman and a boy? The island's owner, and her son, I assume."

Mike vaguely heard the rustle of papers.

"Katrina Denver, widow, twenty-seven years old. In possession of Rock Cay seven years, purchased by James Denver just before his death. Lives quietly; no known liaisons; votes, but attached strongly to neither political party. No criminal record; somewhat active in the Congregational church—life-style as clean as a whistle. Nicknamed the 'Coral Princess' by a number of the main islanders; well liked—"

"And not off the damn island when she was supposed to be!"

Larson was quiet. Mike realized that he was furious at the flub, too, yet he wasn't the one with the victims on his hands. In his hand he had a nice sterile fact-sheet. The military had a complete dossier on her; they just hadn't bothered to make sure she took her sweet rumpus off the island!

"We'll handle the situation on the civilians. Our fault, Taylor. You just continue with your observations. . . ."

Larson kept going; Mike opened his mouth to protest, then gave up. What observations? The whole thing was a mess now. She'd surely sue them. The media would have a heyday.

Wearily, he rubbed his temple, and let Larson try to assure him that the project could be kept classified.

Larson hadn't met his petite little virago—a mother with a totally protective instinct for her son.

"Oh, hell!"

"What was that, Taylor?"

"Nothing. I need a drink."

He didn't even sign out; he just switched off the radio, and stood, swaying a bit. He needed to sleep. But he wanted a drink, and he didn't give a damn about the effects of a whiff of 44DFS when combined with a good shot of Johnnie Walker Black!

He moved to the sink, reached beneath it to the counter, and found the Scotch. He didn't bother with a glass; he just downed a long, long swallow, enough to burn his throat, although the fire in his throat didn't compare with the fire he felt in the rest of his body.

He lifted the bottle in the air dramatically.

"Ah, Dr. Jekyll—meet Mr. Hyde! Tonight, sir, you are a victim of your own mad mind!"

But he wasn't mad, and he damn well knew it. A dreamer or an idealist, maybe. He had learned all about the horrible effects of germ and chemical warfare. And so he'd begun work on a defensive gas that could combat numerous chemical and germ weapons: 44DFS. There were just side effects to it, and they had to be studied and eliminated. He was so close—and now this!

He screwed the cap back on the Scotch. So, her name was Katrina Denver. Well, the hell with the widow Denver.

Mike closed his eyes. He was seeing pink again. A nice cold shower might somehow relieve his tortured masculinity and remind him that he was a scientist tonight, not a hot-blooded man. Then he could lean back at the table and turn on the screens so that he could snooze and watch his unwilling subjects.

Mike reentered the forward sleeping cabin, silently observing Katrina Denver. She was still smiling very sweetly, but her eyes were closed, the covers were up to her throat, and she appeared as innocent as an angel.

He quietly reached into the drawer beneath the bunk and dug out a white terry robe. Seconds later he was standing beneath a spray of ice cold water, rubbing his hands over his face and feeling somewhat better, somewhat relieved. He closed his eyes, smiling suddenly as he wished himself anyplace but where he was. He knew that his sexual stirrings were only a side effect of the drug, but knowing it didn't really change things.

Washington would be nice right now, he thought lazily. Late in the evening. Dinner with Tania. Lovely, warm, giving, totally uninhibited Tania. An independent career woman, one who enjoyed her relationships without clinging, who seemed to understand that his heart was buried. Mmmm. Tania would be just right at this moment. Sleek and naked and passionate and—

"What the—!"

His eyes popped opened and his body tensed as he spun to confront the intruder in his shower. He seized the small hands that were sliding along his ribs.

"Hi!" Katrina said sweetly.

"Oh, God!" Mike groaned.

Her eyes were luminous, sapphire, emerald, swimming with soft and guileless seduction. Her lips were curled into that wonderful, wistful smile. He froze. All that the cold water had done for him, the sight of her undid. She had shed her bathing suit somewhere; she was naked as a nymph and twice as provocative. Her hair flared about her like a siren's temptation, and what little the teal maillot had hidden from him was displayed to him now. She was a full head smaller than he, slim, but proportioned. Her breasts were high and full and rounded; her nipples were the color of rich berries and were less than an inch from his chest. Her waist was tiny; his hands could span it. But then her hips flared out, and her rump was very femininely rounded and in a second he was going to give in to the temptation to cradle his hands there and discover their shape for himself.

She pulled her hands from his grasp and rested them against his chest just below his shoulders. "I was dreaming about you," she whispered, and then she inched toward him. Her lips touched his chest and her belly came in contact with the hard rise of his manhood that he could no longer control.

"Oh, Lord," Mike gasped out as her tongue, warm and sweet as heated honey, raked over his collarbone.

"I was missing you, and you came to me. . . ."

"Oh, Lord!" Mike grated out. His pulse had taken on the beat of the shower, and the ice cold water seemed to steam. He was fire; he was throbbing, aching heat. She had moved against him, nipples raking his chest arousingly, sinuous body sliding along his, her kisses touching him, lower and lower, her whispers silken and sultry and yearning . . .

For another man!

The only thing that pierced the savage tempo of his own desire was the tone of her voice; something in it that hinted of a loss he knew. She had loved once, deeply. And with his drug he had conjured up an image of that love.

Grating his teeth together, he caught her shoulders. He drew her up, he forced her eyes to his. "No!" he yelled at her, shaking her roughly. "No! Listen to me, dammit. I'm not made of stone! This is a drug. You're going to hate me—"

"I couldn't possibly hate you," she interrupted flatly. "I love you."

"No, no, no!"

Exasperated, Mike turned off the water. Soaking wet, he lifted her into his arms, and returned her to her bunk. And then he grinned suddenly, looking down at her perfect form, still aching but now aware of the ironic humor of the situation. "Listen, honey, you glance at me sideways when you're not under the influence, and I'll have you on your back beneath me so fast you'll never know what hit you. That's a promise. But for right now, you've got to go back to sleep."

She smiled, and her eyes closed obediently.

For a moment he remained standing above her. He couldn't totally resist temptation; absently, he stretched out a hand, feathering through the lush strands of hair that tangled in disarray over the pillow. And then his hand was moving again, over her cheek. It was soft. So soft. His knuckles grazed her breast, and then the pure sleek flesh of her abdomen. So delicate, so lovely . . .

"Arggh!"

Swearing against the stupidity of the clod who had put him in his present situation, Mike stamped back to the bathroom and snatched up his robe. It further irritated him to discover that not even the robe could hide his aroused physical state.

He tried to keep his eyes averted from her as he passed back through the cabin, but he couldn't. And he realized that she might be cold. Moving carefully, he clenched his teeth and maneuvered her beneath the covers.

Please, God, he prayed silently, let her sleep the drug off this time!

He left her, carefully closing the door behind him. He reminded himself strictly that he was a scientist and switched on the lab monitors. The boy, he noted from the picture on the tiny screen, was very definitely out like a light.

And she . . . Katrina . . . was sleeping, too, now. As peacefully as an infant.

Mike sighed and decided on one final shot of Johnnie Walker Black. He deserved it. In fact, damn it, he would snooze with the bottle in his arms, for lack of something better.

He procured the bottle and situated himself in the booth that served as the dining table. With his back against the wall he could see the screens, snooze, and surely awake if there was sound or movement from them.

Mike took a sip of the Scotch. He capped it and set it on the varnished wood table. He leaned his head against the wall, closed his eyes, and saw a rush of pink fog.

He opened his eyes and gazed at the screens again. All appeared well; both mother and child were sleeping.

He closed his eyes again. The pink fog encompassed him.

Sleep took him to a place that was beautiful beyond bounds. The sun glowed softly, mingling with the clouds in swirls of crimson and gold. The clouds embraced him; they touched him with a gentle magic, with a tender peace. He was wandering through the clouds, just walking, as if on air. He could see his bare feet touch the floor, never faltering, for there was nothing to injure him in the clouds. He was smiling, and he could feel his smile, just as he could feel the ethereal caress of the clouds against his flesh. He walked naked and serene, knowing that the clouds were gentle, that they were magic.

There was only one disturbance; something that nagged at him, something that tried to reach him. Some thought. Some logical thought. Yet he felt that he was above it; if he didn't allow the thought to pierce the clouds, then it could not, and he could continue to walk, feeling nothing but himself, his smile, his pride to be free and peaceful and strong and alive. . . .

Something touched him. Something more vibrant than the clouds. Something that warmed and thrilled him, and made his blood race like molten lava through him. And there was sound, a whisper that cajoled him, that seduced him, that reminded him just as the touch did that he was a man. . . .

"Come to bed, my love."

To bed.

"Yes . . ."

And he was walking, but no longer alone. She was with him again; the magical pink clouds had brought her back.

"I have missed you so much." The words tore from his throat, touched with joy, touched with agony. There had been many other women, but none who could still the longing, the pain.

She answered with a strangled little cry of her own. "Oh,

yes, I've missed you. It's been so long . . . and I've needed you, and it's been so, so hard to live alone."

She was with him. Standing before him. Touching him, her small hands on his shoulders, her eyes, brimming with tears, locked to his. He grinned crookedly; her eyes were blue. The pink fog had given them a touch of sea-green.

He cupped her chin in his hands and kissed her. Tasted the salt tears on her lips. Sampled their delightful texture. Gently, gently, tenderly, with love . . .

And then it was as if a rush enveloped him, a flood tide of desire. His arms swept around her feverishly; he crushed her length to his, cradling the firm, rounded flesh of her buttocks, lifting her slightly, lifting her to rub her body against the potency of his desire. With hunger he swirled his tongue into her mouth, savoring the sweetness, alive with the tempest of need. She whimpered slightly, but welcomed him, wrapping her arms around him, her fingers playing in the hair at his nape, nails digging into his shoulder at the force of him against her.

He was vital, about to explode. Desperate to love her before she disappeared, yet determined to love her so that she could never forget.

He broke the kiss, allowing her toes to slide back to the floor. Gently he touched her cheeks, and her shoulders. And he bent his head to plant kisses there, to nip lightly at her flesh, to let her feel the graze of his teeth and the moist caress of his tongue. She gasped softly, clinging to his shoulders, and he grinned, the fire inside him growing in heat and wonder with each sweet moan that escaped her throat, telling him of her own need. Her breasts, dear God, how long had it been since he had touched her breasts? He held them, loved them with his hands. Touched one nipple first with a flick of his tongue, suckled the other, tugging at it, savoring the feel and texture in his mouth.

"Ohhhh!" Her teeth, small, delicate, dug tenderly into his shoulders. Her nails skated over his back, raked his buttocks. Each touch brought his heartbeat quicker, the pulse inside him stronger. The need, the hunger, was dizzying.

Erotic, wonderful. Stronger than anything he had known in his life. He wanted to lay her out flat and drive into her, to be shielded in her giving warmth, to have all of her with all of him.

"Oh, please . . ." she gasped out.

He fell to his knees, and the tip of his tongue laved her navel with moist passion. She shook and trembled, and begged him to come to her again. He stroked her thighs and touched them with the heat of his kiss. He slipped his hand between them, enjoying the satin texture of her flesh, questing the heart of her passion, thrilling to the soft cries and moans that shook her. He gripped her hips, holding her still to his hunger and her own, and caressed her with the intimate, intimate heat of his tongue until she gasped out a strangled cry, stiffened and arced like a pagan goddess, and like that goddess, released sweet nectars of love.

He caught her before she could fall and held her in his arms, finding her lips again. She tried to speak around his kisses; she caressed him and touched him. The pink clouds offered them a bed, and he laid her there, coming to her. And again she touched him, exactly where he craved to be touched, her fingers gentle and fervent, her kiss enveloping him, bringing the life and breath of him to thunder. . . .

Then he forced her on her back and rose above her. He wedged his knees between hers; her thighs wound around him in a silken embrace, as welcoming as the velvet embrace of her body, as the cry that escaped her in another startled gasp, as her promise to love and need him forever. . . .

At that moment he knew that he was flesh and blood, that he was a man loving a woman, that his body strained and dampened and soared at a frantic, pulsing beat. Yet the pink clouds were all around him, adding magic.

She, too, was real. Real and beautiful, seductive and sinuous, impassioned and so wonderfully sensuous. She was a part of him, so feminine, so fine, hips fluidly rotating, arching, again and again. . . .

The pleasure, the climax, was an explosion of his being, so good that it hurt, touching the world with a streak of golden light that shattered the clouds. He was drenched; he was sated. He held her, pressing her to him, speaking breathless, soothing whispers as they drifted slowly down from the pinnacle in another silken cloud of fulfillment. He felt that he was with her still, inside of her, a part of her. And indeed, he knew that he had filled her. With himself, with all of himself.

He stroked her hair. He whispered. She whispered. He vaguely mused that her hair had grown quite long while they had been parted.

It wasn't until hours later—hours, or moments?—that he awoke again. Awoke with a painfully lucid mind and perfect reason.

Reason that clearly and dismayingly told him that the hair tangled around his shoulders wasn't just long—it was deep, dark red.

And it belonged to Katrina Denver. Just like the face that nestled against his chest, and the long, slim, naked leg that was cast over his own muscled, hairy, naked thigh.

CHAPTER TWO

Oh, hell.

Oh, *hell.*

If this damn situation wasn't going from ridiculously bad to worse.

Mike closed his eyes and cast his wrist over his forehead, praying that he could awake all over again and discover that the petite redhead was a 44DFS illusion.

He opened his eyes again. She was no illusion. Nor had she been an illusion in the night. Only the love had been an illusion, the belief in magic.

Not the act of love, logic warned him. That had been very, very real. So real that he could still warm to the touch of her, remember with aching clarity the sweet, wild things that had gone on between them. . . .

He cursed aloud, then carefully tried to unravel her hair from his shoulders. What would she remember, he wondered. His own recall was perfect, but then he hadn't inhaled half of what she had of the drug. She had acted out a dream, and perhaps she would awake believing only in that dream. He still didn't know all the repercussions of the drug. It had been tested on rats, rabbits, beagles, chimps, and fighting cocks, but never human beings before.

He winced; it shouldn't have been tested on humans now. And sure as hell not in these circumstances!

She'd wanted to see him hanged before; now she'd want to perform the execution herself.

If she remembered.

Oh, God! What the hell had he done!

Carefully, he untangled her leg from his. He stood, then stared blankly at the blackness beyond the porthole. And then he looked down at her again, shaking his head slightly, a soft smile curling his lips.

He was horribly in the wrong. Yet who could resist dreams? Who could resist such a balm to the soul?

"Thank you," he whispered, and with great tenderness he moved a wild strand of her hair from her cheek to the pillow. "I'll never be able to say this when you're awake, but what you gave me was more, much, much more, than 44DFS. It was something very fine. Something I haven't known in more than a decade—"

He broke off, quickly. She was stirring, her thick lashes fluttering over her eyes. His breath caught, but she merely murmured something and nestled into the pillow.

Michael took a deep, shaky breath. He needed some good strong coffee now, something to completely clear his head, something that would let him think.

He needed to decide just what to say and do when she awoke. Ethically, he felt he had to be honest. Yet something inside warned him that she might not want to know the truth.

He ducked down by the bed, pulling out his drawer. He didn't even know where his robe was, but it didn't matter. He wanted to dress in uniform whites for morning. If nothing else, he was definitely going to have to discover what she was still doing on the island when she had signed a government form promising to be off it! And then, he was going to have to give her some kind of explanation, if not a complete one.

Just as his hand closed around a pair of socks, her fingers fell on his shoulder. "James?"

Her voice was husky, full of pain and yearning.

He rose, taking her hands, leaning over her.

"Go to sleep, Katrina."

"No!" The agonized sound of her cry closed around him. She shook her head, a haze of tears glittering in her eyes.

"You have to sleep; I have to go—"

She was halfway up, wrapping her arms around him. She buried her face against his shoulder, and she trembled slightly as a sob threatened to engulf her.

"No, no! You're here . . . you're here, and I'm afraid to close my eyes because you'll disappear."

Her breasts were against him, soft, full, and feminine. It was nearly impossible to ignore the plea in her voice.

He wasn't under the influence of 44DFS anymore.

But he was still human, and torn in two.

"Go to sleep, Katrina," he told her firmly, pressing her back to the bed. "Sleep. . . ."

At last her eyes closed, and he left her.

Katrina awoke very slowly, and oddly enough, the sensation was pleasant enough—at first.

It was very much as if a soft, soft billow of clouds had pressed her forward to some sort of landing, then faded, billowing just as gently away and out of reach. She opened her eyes and saw a paneled wall alien to her memory. Yet even as she realized she was someplace where she shouldn't be, she still felt serene. It was as if she had come from a never-never land where dreams could be real, where everything was happiness, where a person was embraced and cherished and loved.

Really loved, she thought abruptly, frowning then. And then she blushed to the roots of her hair, remembering the details of her dreams. Never had she dreamed so vividly.

Her frown became a wince; she closed her eyes once again. She had been dreaming about James by the pool—not so much dreaming, really, but daydreaming, remembering. Had she been so lonely, so lost, that she had conjured such a memory, and tossed and turned alone, envisioning him with her?

Her eyes flew open; all the gentle curves and billows of the pink clouds were gone completely, and she experienced a terrible sensation of pitching and swaying. And facts, not dreams, flooded her mind.

Jason had called her, and she had run to the sound of his

voice. And at the southern pool she had come into contact with a maniac in a spacesuit, passed out cold, and then—

She jerked up and stared wildly around herself. The pitching and swaying must mean that she was in some kind of a boat or ship.

Jason! Where was her son?

Katrina practically flew out of the bed, ready to fly into battle, to scream and rant and rave and lash out in panic and fear until she found him.

Her hand touched the door lever, and then, only then, did she pause, completely stunned.

She was naked.

A flush crimsoned her face, and then her entire naked body. She didn't know whether to be terrified, furious, humiliated, or all three. But as desperate as she was about her son, she didn't want to go flying out of the privacy of the cabin in her present state.

Her teal maillot was on the floor at the foot of the bed, still damp. She shimmied into it breathlessly, quickly decided it wasn't enough, then noticed a worn terry robe on the floor beyond it. She grabbed the robe; it was way too big for her, but that made her very happy, since it encompassed a good three quarters of her body.

She tied the belt around her waist and hurriedly rolled up the sleeves, then suddenly paused again, frowning as she looked around the surprisingly roomy cabin.

There was really nothing there. A small dresser, a smaller closet, and the bunk. There were no pictures on the wall, just the gleaming paneling.

On the dresser, though, were a few items that set her heart to a miserable pounding: after-shave, a comb, a man's tortoiseshell brush, a set of gold cuff-links, and an expensive black-banded diver's watch. A new panic filled her senses. Where in hell was she? Who was the strange man in the silver spacesuit who had accosted her, yelling at her for being on her own damned property!

She turned around in a fury, ready to grip the door and fling it open with a vengeance. Something stopped her—a sense of confusion that made her turn and survey the ten-by-ten space one more time.

The cabin was very neat. Beneath the men's paraphernalia, the cherry wood dresser set gleamed. Curtains in white and chocolate covered the porthole, and the floor was spotless. Only the bed—a handsome bunk tacked to the starboard side—was a mess, the sheets all twisted and awry, as if she had, indeed, lived out her erotic dreams.

"No," she murmured aloud. And she had awakened stark naked. . . .

She didn't dare think. But she did find herself walking to the bunk and fingering the sheets.

They had been very clean; she even recognized the scent of the detergent on them, because it was the one she used herself. But there was another scent to them, something subtle and musky, like cologne mingled with the scent of freshly bathed flesh. Male flesh. . . .

The boat pitched suddenly, sending her crashing back to the bunk. Katrina stood, loath to touch the sheets, loath to think. She had been alone, she told herself. She had been alone—she had been . . .

Dammit! She had been drugged; it was the only explanation.

And Jason must have been drugged too. Jason! Katrina winced, swinging about again, sick that she had been worried about such a trivial thing as how she'd spent the night when she still hadn't seen her son, didn't have any idea of where he might be.

She stormed out the door, ready to scream, frightened despite herself, and bracing for whatever she might see. She stepped out of the cabin, ferociously yelling, "Where is my son! What in God's name is going on here?"

Her voice seemed to echo down the hall, which was flanked on the starboard side first by a dining table and overhead cabinets, then by a large and handsomely carved chart desk. Across from that desk was a well-equipped galley; down from the galley—near her—was a long Formica shelf and more cabinets.

The Formica table set her into panic all over again. There were all kinds of test tubes there, set carefully in holders, labeled meticulously. And right above the table were three little screens that appeared to be televisions.

Narrowing her eyes, Katrina took a step closer to them, then gasped. One was blank. One gave a picture of the cabin she had just vacated. And in the other, she saw Jason, sprawled out comfortably on a nice big bunk, a smile on his lips as he slept.

She gathered the oversized robe to her throat. Jason! She touched the screen, tears in her eyes. Jason, Jason, Jason! He seemed to be okay. She just had to reach him.

Oh, God! They had been kidnapped by a maniac. . . .

"Good morning, Mrs. Denver. Coffee?"

Letting out a little screech at the sound of the deep male voice, Katrina spun around, bracing herself against the table. She thought it would be the silver-eyed stranger in the spacesuit once again.

He had silver eyes, all right. Silver and steel. He stood on the bottom rung of the three steps that led to the deck, but he was clad in white slacks and a white short-sleeved shirt with some kind of epaulets on the shoulders.

He even wore a white, blue-rimmed cap, with some kind of insignia on it.

She realized dimly that he was a tall man, at least a good foot taller than she was. He appeared lean but not really slim. His shoulders were broad beneath the white cotton shirt, but his waist was slim and his hips were narrow.

He was well tanned, and his eyes were vivid against the bronze of his features. It struck her that he was a very handsome man, although not in the conventional sense. His mouth was generous, his jaw square, and his cheekbones were high and broad. He was clean shaven, with neatly cropped tawny hair feathering beneath his cap. His nose was long and straight. There were faint lines around his eyes and mouth, telling her that he was probably around forty. The power of his physique and the rugged appeal of his face startled her.

When she didn't answer, he moved casually to the stove, where he proceeded to pour himself a cup of coffee.

Michael watched her warily. Damn her; he felt so guilty, he couldn't even find the words to be polite to her! He tried to rationalize that his guilt was her fault for not leaving the island but that only made him feel more guilty!

Katrina stared at him incredulously for a moment, then flew at him in a snarling burst of fury.

He saw her coming, and quickly set the coffee down. He might deserve a good slap in the face, but he sure as hell didn't feel like being scalded—not when she had refused to get off the island!

He caught her, then held her at arm's length as she tried wildly to slash and kick him. Did she remember more than he had suspected? he wondered grimly.

"Stop it—" he began, but just as suddenly as she had flown at him, she wrenched away from him, although she was still eying him with the look of a wary tigress prepared to go to battle again. She was almost comical—her hair a mane about her, his robe ridiculously large on her small frame.

She didn't apologize for her attempted assault. Fists clenched at her side, she grated out venomously, "Who the hell are you, and what is going on here?"

"Captain Taylor, Mrs. Denver. Dr. Taylor, if you prefer. I'm with the Navy—"

"What Navy?" she shouted furiously.

He paused, drawing a deep breath. "The United States Navy, Mrs. Denver. Now—"

"Our Navy? I swear to you, Captain, Doctor—whatever you are!—that someone will pay for this! Since when do the Armed Forces have the right to abduct civilians? Has there been a military coup here?"

She didn't give him a chance to answer, but raged on.

"Someone is going to pay for this, Taylor." She pointed her forefinger at him. *"You* are going to pay for this! Oh! I don't even know if I believe you! Since when does the Navy send men to small islands in spacesuits? Why are we in this boat? Where is my son? If you don't bring me to him this instant, you'll find yourself in a mangler, you—you maniac!"

Katrina was amazed that after all her righteous threats he had the bloody nerve to stare at her with total irritation, then turn back to the stove to retrieve his coffee cup.

"I—"

"You just saw your son on the screen, Mrs. Denver. You know perfectly well that he is sleeping comfortably. Now I repeat, would you like some coffee?"

"Coffee," Katrina repeated. "At a time like this, in a situation like this, you're offering me *coffee?*"

He shifted slightly, leaning against the counter, studying her casually over the rim of his mug. "It is a customary morning drink," he grated out, and she realized then that beneath the surface he was as uncomfortable as she was.

"Oh!" she raged out in frustration. If only she could hit him! One good, walloping belt across that stubborn, square jaw . . .

He sighed at last and set his cup down. "Mrs. Denver, I would tell you how sorry I am that you became involved in this, except that in your present state of agitation—"

"Agitation? I'm not agitated, I'm furious! I'm irate! I'm—"

"I repeat, Mrs. Denver, I'm very sorry about your involvement. Now, if you'd like some coffee, we can sit down at the table and try to discuss this like rational adults."

"Rational . . ." She wanted to swear again, to strike out in her confusion and the fear that remained with her still. But suddenly, tears stung her eyes; she still hadn't seen Jason, hadn't been able to hold him, to assure herself that he really was sleeping, that he would awake happy and well.

Her gaze inadvertently switched to the Formica table with all its test tubes. She still might be dealing with a madman dressed up in a Navy uniform. It just might be best to humor him along. . . .

"I'll—I'll have some coffee," she said as pleasantly as she could manage. "If you'll promise to take me to my son as soon as we've talked."

He turned to procure another cup. For a brief moment Katrina entertained the idea of reaching for something and cracking it over his head.

He turned back to her with a warning in his smile, as if he had read her mind.

"Sugar, Mrs. Denver?"

She shook her head. Forget force; she could never compete with him in the brawn department.

He lifted the cup to her, indicating the table against the starboard wall. "There's milk in the refrigerator if you'd like."

She nodded and very nervously opened the small door beneath her. She blanched then; the milk was in a test tube.

She slammed the door shut, grating her teeth at his smooth grin. "You did that on purpose!"

"No, I didn't. But you seem to want me to be Dr. Frankenstein—maybe I'm just trying to oblige."

"Oblige my foot!" Katrina muttered as he moved past her to set the cups on the table.

Katrina felt little chills of unease slip down her spine. When he had been near, she'd felt a sense of déjà vu. There'd been something about him that was so familiar. His scent, perhaps: a subtle after-shave, fresh and like the air after a storm—

And just like that pleasant, lingering scent in the cabin, on the sheets. . . .

She shook herself vehemently. It was obviously his cabin. The damned after-shave was sitting on his dresser.

"Quite honestly, Mrs. Denver, it's just milk. The container broke, and I had to put it in something."

Katrina rose, bringing the glass vial with her. She slid into a chair across from him. "Milk—and what else?" she inquired with a saccharine smile.

"Just milk," he repeated.

She stirred milk into her coffee uneasily.

She was somewhat surprised when he pulled a pack of cigarettes from his top white shirt pocket, and lit one, inhaling as he watched her, almost as if he were as nervous as she was. His eyes, steely gray this morning, seemed to penetrate into her soul.

"I'm waiting—"

"For an explanation, yes." He inhaled, then swore softly as the coffee cups slid across the table at another lurch of the boat. He caught his cup; she caught hers.

"How are you feeling this morning, Mrs. Denver?" he asked her suddenly, and once again she felt that she was being carefully observed—more so than just physically.

And her strange dreams rose to the forefront of her mind, causing her to bow her head slightly and as she replied a bit curtly, "Fine." Then she added, "How am I supposed to feel?"

He waved a hand nonchalantly in the air. "Fine. Rested. Happy. Are you all of those things, Mrs. Denver?"

"You're forgetting, I'm irate. And I'm supposed to be asking the questions."

"Shoot. I'll answer what I can."

"What you can!"

"All right, all right. Let me start, and we'll see where it leads. Mrs. Denver, you were supposed to be off that island—"

"I own the island!"

"I know—but you signed a government consent form to leave it for the period of a week. And you were compensated for that time. I know that you were sent a check, because I signed the draft myself. And I've spoken to the base; they guarantee me that they have your signature on the consent form."

Katrina inhaled sharply. "I—I did rent out the island, to the government. But I was called—at least three weeks ago—and told that another site had been chosen for the 'exercises'!"

He frowned sharply. "Nothing was ever changed, Mrs. Denver."

She sipped her coffee, staring at him warily. The uniform looked real. . . .

He smiled, very much aware of her scrutiny. "I assure

you, Mrs. Denver, I am a captain with the Navy. The U.S. Navy. I am an M.D., and I also have a doctorate in chemistry. What happened—"

"You don't look so smart," she interrupted.

He laughed, and she thought again that he was a striking man. He had the rugged, outdoors type of face that looked its very best when twisted into a grin.

"I'm not at all sure if that's a compliment or an insult, Mrs. Denver. And, I didn't claim to be smart." A silvery light of amusement was in his eyes and it seemed that he leaned a little closer to her. "The degrees are real, though; I'm licensed to be a Frankenstein, at any rate. But, Mrs. Denver, I swear to you, the plans were never changed."

"Someone called me!"

"It had to have been a crank."

"It couldn't have been—I never told anyone I had rented the island."

"But I'm telling you, it was never called off. And there were Marine officers who went to the island to make sure it was clear!"

Katrina stiffened, bringing her back against the booth. "Maybe this is irrelevant at the moment. What were you doing there?" she demanded fiercely.

He shrugged. "You know what I was doing. Testing a—a gas."

"Go on."

"That's it. In a nutshell."

"I don't want it in a damned nutshell!" Katrina exploded. "I want to know what this drug is; I want to know why my son is still sleeping, I want to know what—what—"

She was red with fury, and Mike sighed, well aware that she wanted to know what had made her experience the very strange sensations of her "dreams."

"Mrs. Denver, that's all I can tell you. Except that I can assure that there are absolutely no aftereffects of this substance. Jason will awake perfectly fine and normal—excited, probably, because he will have dreamed about a great space adventure or something like that."

"A space adventure?"

He smiled uneasily. "That's one of the side effects of the drug, Mrs. Denver. Under its influence one dreams pleasant, pleasant dreams. Dreams that live out fantasies, and delve straight to the secret desires in our hearts."

"Why—oh, why?—couldn't she control the color that flooded into her face. He was watching her with such humor and curiosity. Did he know, then . . . know the nature of her night? Know that she had been adrift in pink clouds of sensuality, that she had envisioned James coming back to hold her . . .

And much, much more?

Her eyes flashed to her left, to the television screens. On the one, Jason still slept. And on the other, she could still see the tousled bunk where she had slept. Yes, damn it! He knew things, he had watched her all night, he had invaded her privacy with no thought of consent; he had seen her as she had slept, naked and bare and tossing and—

"How dare you!" she screamed suddenly, and her hand lashed out across the table in a split second of fury so explosive it could not be contained.

His reaction was strange; very strange. He could have stopped her from striking him, but he didn't. He allowed her stinging blow to fall against his cheek, and then he merely rose, absently rubbing his face.

"I'm sorry, Mrs. Denver," he said softly. "Truly, I am. I can't tell you any more about the drug; it's still considered top secret—its properties are classified information."

Whether it was ego, pride, or the sense that she had been violated somehow, Katrina could not let it drop. She believed him—his story was too fantastic to have been made up!—but she couldn't accept what had happened.

"Correction—captain, doctor, whatever you like to be called. What you did was irresponsible and dangerous! You had no right to intrude on private lives! I intend to sue you, the Navy, and the entire damn government! This—"

"This!" He thundered suddenly in returning, spinning back to slam his cup against the table as he eyed her with a silver fury to match her own, his knuckles white where they gripped the mug, "This is bigger than any of your petty little hang-ups, Mrs. Denver! You have a responsibility! Your signature is on an important form, and only an idiot would think one phone call could cancel the whole deal! But you just go ahead, you sue whoever you damn please! You can talk to every newspaper in the country. But I'd be careful, if I were you. Maybe the state will think that a woman who didn't bother to take her son from an experimental site—after giving her consent for its use!—isn't a fit mother.

Katrina was confused, furious, and guilt ridden. Tears were stinging at her eyes; she was lost and flailing and she wanted nothing more than to see him disappear into the ocean. She raised a hand again, desperately wishing she could do him some real physical harm, repay him for what he had done to her, to Jason, to—

"Oohh!" she screamed out, but this time, when her hand moved, he wasn't feeling so benevolent. He caught it, twisting it behind her back, bringing her against his chest . . . tightly. Eyes as hard as steel burned into her; she felt the rigid, rigid strength and control in his body, and though she tried to twist away in fear and horror, she could not. He shook her, causing her to cry out again.

And then his hold eased, but he did not release her.

"Just let me go!" she screamed out desperately. "Give me my son, and let me go! It's happened, and now it's over, and all I want to do is get away—"

"I can't let you go, not until this evening. And I guarantee you—"

"What the hell do you think this is, a communist state?"

"If it were a communist state, Mrs. Denver, we could probably just shoot you and quit worrying about confidential information being broadcast coast to coast!"

"Let me go!"

His eyes narrowed dangerously. "I am in the military, Mrs. Denver. There has been a terrible mistake. You have been wronged—how, I don't understand, but I'm very sorry.

But I'm also tired of being abused by a self-righteous little shrew—"

"And I am tired of being used by an insane chemist who seems to think that he's God!"

Her heart was beating wildly against her chest as he held her; her throat was tilted all the way back so that she was forced to meet his eyes. That scent of his, of freshness and air and the sea and a breeze and—and rugged, insinuative masculinity!—was all around her, as was the horrible sense of déjà vu. She felt as if she had been here before, as if she knew him, as if she had stroked his handsome cheeks and rested against the rippling, heated muscles in his chest, as if she knew the touch of his long bronzed fingers, knew his very heartbeat, the sound of his voice in a whisper . . .

Knew . . . and liked . . .

She stiffened, but offered no resistance. Her eyes fell, and she shuddered with the force of her sudden confusion and misery. It had been almost five years since she had been held, even like this. And the sensation seemed to call to her. She wanted to like him, she even wanted to burst into tears and lean against him.

"Please let me go," she said, calling upon all the soft dignity she could muster.

He released her instantly, then spoke with a depth of sorrow she could not deny. "I'm sorry, Mrs. Denver. Really sorry. But I can't answer any more of your questions. Not about the drug."

He walked away from her, gazing, with a frown, up the short steps to the deck and the sky above. Katrina barely noticed him. There was just one more question that she had to ask.

"Captain?"

"What?" he asked a little absently.

She approached him, her hands set stubbornly on her hips, her voice steady despite the color that again flooded her whole being.

"I awoke—unclothed. Did you—did you take my bathing suit off?"

He stared at her blankly. "Pardon?"

"You heard me!"

He opened his mouth as if to answer; static suddenly filled the air. His mocking gaze left her and he rushed to the radio.

"44DFS here—come in, base, base. Dammit, come in!"

The static faded and died. With an exclamation of disgust he threw the receiver down and turned back to her, his arms crossed over his chest.

"It seems you have communications problems, Captain!" she snapped. "You don't know a damned thing about what you're doing, you idiot!"

He stiffened; she heard the grate of his teeth. He stared at her then, and smiled politely.

"Ah, but I do know what I'm doing—and not doing, Mrs. Denver. And, no, I did not take your suit off you. You performed that lovely little strip-tease all by yourself."

CHAPTER THREE

"Mom?"

Jason's voice—soft and a little awed as it came to her from the television screen—sent Katrina spinning around, momentarily heedless of anything else.

"Jason?"

She looked first to the screen, then to the steel-eyed captain with an expression that promised murder if she wasn't brought instantly to her son.

"I'd like to advise that you don't upset him unduly," he warned, then started past her, toward the stern.

Katrina followed him quickly—through the cabin where she had spent the night, then through a second door, next to the head, one that blended nicely into the paneling. They went through another door to a pleasant cabin, this one lined with windows that looked out onto the dreary gray day.

Katrina noticed briefly that the yacht was now pitching and weaving constantly; yesterday's breeze had obviously whipped into a wind and the sea was churning.

But it didn't mean a thing to her—not then. Jason was all that mattered. Holding him again, touching him, assuring herself that he was really and truly fine.

"Jason!"

He was sitting up in the bed, smiling, looking around with awe. He grinned first at Mike, who hung back. Katrina sped past him, raced to the bunk, and wrapped her arms around her son.

He hugged her back, but just barely. Jason was eight years

old; a very independent eight, all boy, and at the stage where such an expression of affection from one's mother was just a little bit embarrassing.

"Mom . . ." he murmured, squirming. But then his hands were on her shoulders and he was looking at her with eager fascination in his eyes. Dark eyes, like his father's. His slightly long, ruffled hair, though, carried her deep glint of red.

"Wow!" he said. "What is this place?"

"Jason, are you all right?" Katrina was not about to be deterred. She reached out to move his hair from his forehead, anxiously studying his eyes. He looked fine, absolutely normal.

"Mo-om!" he protested. And then his eyes fell on Mike again. "Are you the spaceman?"

Mike laughed easily. "Sorry, son. I'm not a spaceman. I'm with the Navy."

"Oh," Jason said, disappointed. "Well that's neat, I guess."

Mike left his position near the door to approach the bed, smiling. He gazed at Katrina; he saw the stubborn set of her jaw and the purse of her lips, and his smile tightened grimly as he indicated that she should move.

She didn't.

He reached for Jason's wrist anyway and she lowered her head, heartily resentful but also aware of the fact that he was a physician, albeit an unorthodox one. With a soft sigh of impatience she moved. Mike took her position at Jason's side.

Katrina stared out the window at the dead gray day. There was silence for a minute, then Jason—never good at keeping quiet—began to talk.

"Are you absolutely sure that you're not a spaceman? I had this dream—it was the neatest dream I've ever had!—about being in space. I had this thing called a star cruiser. R2-D2 was there, and Hans Solo, and you were in it too! Oh, not like you are now; you were in your space suit, of course! You were really from a planet called Vitrian, but you'd joined forces with Earth to help wipe out the deadly Odites, who were at war against the Federation. We all went into battle together—"

"And we won, I hope?" Mike inquired.

"Well, of course, we won!" Jason exclaimed happily. "It was just great!"

"And you remember it all—clearly?" he asked him.

"Clear as glass!" Jason laughed. He went on about the Odites while Katrina longed to tie a muzzle around his mouth. What had happened to him? Jason was a great kid—polite, but very wary of strangers. But to Mike, Jason was talking nonstop, just as if he'd known the man all of his life.

"Tell me everything, Jason. From the time I saw you at the pool. From the time you came to me."

"Will you stop it! This is madness!" Katrina swung back around to face them, in a rage.

Both Mike and her son stared at her with annoyance, as if it were she who was completely mad.

Jason appeared perplexed. "Mom, it's okay—"

"Captain Taylor, may I see you? Alone, please!" Her eyes widened to stress the last word.

Mike and Jason exchanged a glance and a shrug, which irritated her even further. "Be right back, Jason," Taylor promised; then he was on his feet. He bowed slightly—with definite sarcasm—to indicate that she might precede him out of the cabin.

Katrina did so. She didn't stop beneath the sheltered leeway, but stomped up the starboard steps to reach the deck. She didn't look at Mike, but gripped the wooden railing—both for something on which to vent the fury and strength that ripped through her arms, and because the yacht was dipping and swaying quite precariously.

She heard him behind her. He had sat down on the center rise that was actually the roof of Jason's cabin.

She didn't turn around. She didn't want to look at him.

"You know, Taylor, I really am trying to be calm about this whole thing. I still have no proof that you're not a maniac. I'm giving you the benefit of the doubt because I have no choice. All right, you're Navy, and you're a doctor. And according to you we stumbled into your drug. But I won't be used! Nor do I want my son used. He is *not* one of your laboratory rats, and I will not have him become one! You're not going to sit there and pry and pick his mind! He's a little boy, not—not something for you to study!"

He didn't answer her. Katrina was forced to turn around, and as she did, the sea suddenly swelled, making the boat keel toward the port side.

She might as well have run to him, so cleanly was she swept from her position and catapulted into his arms.

And he was ready. Reflexes quick and attuned to the caprices of the sea, he caught her. Arms strong and sure and steadying as she landed within them, face first, into his chest. Katrina gasped against the surprising force of the elements, and as she struggled to regain the breath wrenched from her, hot sparks danced along her spine. When he held her . . . when she was close . . . it was there again. A sense of déjà vu, as if she knew him well. The nice, nice male scent of him, the ripple of his muscle. Even the tender amusement in his eyes when she raised her head and found him watching her. . . .

"Oh! Let go of me!"

He released her, and she started to fall. Instinctively, she grasped for him again. And he smiled again, fingers curling around her arms as he led her down beside him.

"I think," he murmured, watching her, "that we've a bigger problem at hand at the moment."

"What could be—"

He rose very steady on well-trained sea legs. Staring off into the gray horizon, he shook his head. "I don't like this weather. Do you?"

For the first time Katrina really gave her attention to the day. Whitecaps were forming; rain was definitely in the air. She couldn't see the color of the clouds, because everything around her was dull gray, and darkening.

"We can't stay out here," she said flatly. "If this isn't a

true tropical storm forming, it's at least going to be one hell of a severe gale!"

"I know," he murmured a little absently. Then he was gone, back down the companionway. Katrina raced a little breathlessly after his long strides through the storage compartment, the sleeping cabin, and into the galley. He was at the chart desk, at the radio, identifying himself over and over again at 44DFS.

All he received in return was static.

An oath escaped him as he threw the earphones down on the desk, removed his cap, and threaded his fingers wearily through his hair.

Then he glanced at Katrina, as if just realizing that she was there, silently and warily standing behind him. "You got any kind of a safe harbor on that island of yours?"

"Just the beach—that's the most protected area."

"It's surrounded by reefs."

"Yes, it is," Katrina said. "But if you know what you're doing . . ." She shrugged. "There is no dockage, though. All you can do is take her into the cove, anchor, and hope for the best."

He seemed to mull over her words, watching her distrustfully. Then he stood, approaching her with a little smile. "Why do I get the feeling that you'd love to see the *Maggie Mae* in a thousand pieces?"

Katrina was tempted to back away from him. There was still a fury burning deep inside her; he'd no right to play God with them! And she still didn't know . . . didn't understand . . . everything that had happened.

She didn't like the feeling that she wanted to like him, to touch him, to laugh with him. She even had the wistful feeling that she would like to get to know him very, very well.

He was an attractive man, she reminded herself stiffly. Very attractive, and painfully beguiling to her, although she didn't know exactly why. Except that he was so tall, so nicely muscled, so lean. Everything about him spoke of the differences in the sexes, differences she had forgotten for years now, so determined had she been to live in the past.

James—who had been too young to die. James, whom she had loved from the very first time she had ever seen him, sitting astride his motorcycle, looking at her in such a way that her heart had seemed to melt, her insides to go ragged. . . .

Katrina turned away from Taylor abruptly, tears stinging her eyes. What had she done to herself? she wondered with dismay. Set herself apart from life for so long that when this stranger abruptly tore into privacy and dreams, she had lost all sense of reason? Surely if she had just dated now and then, she wouldn't feel all these rather humiliating and rather desperate sensations now!

"I've no intention of hurting your precious ship!" she lashed out. She spun back around, ready again to do battle. "Nor am I your prisoner. There's definitely a storm brewing out there—strong enough to clog your pathetic excuse for a radio. If you want your ship safely in, I'll pilot her for you. If not, I'm taking my son back home so that we can batten down."

"I'll take her in. Now," he said stiffly. "And you're not running off with my dinghy, because I've things that have to be salvaged off this boat!"

With an abrupt and very militaristic about-face, he left her standing there and quickly clambered up the few steps to the deck. A second later she heard him swearing softly. Then he came down the steps, drenched.

He shot her one of his level silver glances—as if it had been entirely her fault that the rain had already started. He dug into a cabinet beneath the chart desk and procured a couple of yellow slickers, tossing her one.

"Well?"

"Well, what?"

"Do you intend to let me know where these reefs lie, or not?"

She shrugged slowly. "Sure. But you should know that I still intend to sue you and everyone else I can think of, and to speak to every reporter I can find this side of the Mason-Dixon line."

"Don't waste your time," he told her briefly. "Go straight for the *National Enquirer.* They'll give you top billing."

He was back on the deck again. Katrina followed him, staggering a little against the sudden force of the wind and the pelting rain. She hadn't been afraid before—now she was. She was accustomed to the weather; she had seen the water rise and churn many times before. But staring beyond portside, she could dimly see her small island, Rock Cay. The palms were already being flattened by the force of the wind.

It was difficult to stand. Katrina wound her fingers around the cabin door frame.

"It's bad!" she yelled out. "You need to hurry!"

He grunted something, busy winding the winch to pull in the anchor. Beneath the rain and the slicker she could see the workings of his broad shoulders, and for a moment a thought chilled her.

What if he had been a maniac? She had always felt safe and comfortable on the island, closed off in their own private world. There was no crime on Rock Cay. Jason went into Islamorada by motor launch for school, and they had friends there as well. There were the tourists, and there were the islanders, and everything was always easy.

But if this stranger had been a maniac, a criminal—what would she have done? she wondered with dismay. He was a head taller than she, and probably had a hundred pounds over her. She could have never fought him. And then, what of Jason?

Jason . . . still back in the cabin, alone.

Ignoring Taylor, Katrina raced back through the yacht and burst in on her son again. He was kneeling on the bunk, watching the weather with avid enthusiasm and a certain wisdom.

"Man, is it blowing! Is this going to be a hurricane?"

Katrina shook her head. "I don't know, Jason. But listen to me. We're going to try and get into the cove. Stay here until I call you, okay? Then we'll have to take the dinghy, or maybe even swim into shore. And, Jase, the water is going to be really rough. It—"

"Currents, Mom, I know." He sighed with a patience that belied his years. Then he grinned at her a little crookedly, softening his words. "Quit worrying about me. I'm almost as big as you are and I'm actually a better swimmer."

"Well!" Katrina said, but then she laughed, even if the laugh was a little nervous. "You may be the better swimmer, but you're going to listen to me, young man. You may be almost as big but you're not bigger than I am. And I am worried, so take heed—okay?"

He nodded. She started to hurry back, but he called her.

"Don't worry, Mom. *He*'s here."

"That's half of why I'm worried," Katrina muttered, and Jason chuckled; the sound, again, was disturbingly old for his youth.

"I like him. We'll be okay."

"How can you like him or dislike him?" Katrina asked irritably. "You've only known him a short time."

"No," Jason protested. "I conquered the Odites with him."

"That was a dream, Jason."

"Maybe. But you don't need to be with someone long to know if you like him or not. You just know."

Katrina hadn't the time or energy to argue with such logic. She raised a brow, left the cabin, and clambered straight up the side stairs to the deck.

The *Maggie Mae* was a three-masted sailing yacht, but like most such vessels, she had been supplied with a motor. Her sails were all neatly furled and tied; Mike, bareheaded now against the lash of the rain, was already behind the round, wood-spiked wheel.

The motor was humming briskly, and they were headed toward the beach on the island.

Katrina had to cling to the mainmast to reach him. She had just sat down at his side before they keeled port again, sending her crashing against his shoulder.

"Where the hell have you been?" he demanded harshly,

barely aware that she was straining to balance away from him.

"I went to see my son!" she snapped back.

He grunted out something, then said, "All right—we're almost there! What the hell am I doing?"

He was shouting; she shouted, too, in order to be heard above the growl of the motor and the howl of the wind and sea.

"If you'd just give me the damn wheel—"

"Nothing doing!"

"You admit you haven't the faintest idea of what—"

"I've been on ships since you were in grade school, lady! Now just point out the—"

"You've been on ships, but not here! Give me the wheel—"

She reached for it; too late. They both heard the long, tearing scrape against the hull, like the sound of nails scraping over a blackboard—amplified. It was a sound that would have assured even a complete landlubber that the *Maggie Mae* had been hit, and badly.

"Now look what you've done!" Katrina exclaimed.

"What I've done! Dammit! I should have known you were out to destroy everything!"

"Destroy! If you would have—"

"Oh, shut up—and get Jason!"

Oh, God, yes, Jason!

Katrina was up with one last, backward epithet for him. She was only dimly aware that he was up, too, headed for the port.

Jason—no fool—was already out of the cabin and scampering up the stairs. "We hit, huh." It was a statement, not a question.

"Yeah—" And Katrina had a few things to say about Mike being an idiot. The wind and rain swallowed most of her words as she grabbed his hand, the two of them slipping and swaying together as they hurried over the deck by way of grasping the mast.

She didn't see Mike anywhere; the deck itself appeared to

be gray, the wind had risen to such a lash that the rain wasn't just falling, it was being hurtled at them in sheets.

"Here! The dinghy."

Almost blinded, Katrina stumbled that way. She was soaked to the bone. Even with the wind, it wasn't cold, but the feeling of being so very wet was miserable and chilling. Jason, she realized, had nothing on but his trunks, and yet he was probably just as well off, since nothing was protection against the onslaught.

Mike was struggling to hold the dinghy next to the *Maggie Mae.* "Come on!" He urged her.

"Jason—go!" Katrina said to her son, glad then that he was agile, that he was accustomed to boats and water, that he was a little boy full of ability, independence, and coordination. Still, she steadied him when he leapt to the rim with his bare feet.

Mike caught his body and set him into the one of the seats. Then he looked back to Katrina.

She, too, balanced onto the rim, comfortable with her own coordination. But just then a gust of wind sheeted against her with enormous strength and she plummeted back to the deck of the *Maggie Mae,* the breath knocked from her, her head spinning. Water filled her mouth instantly, and she choked, tears stinging her eyes.

She hadn't seen him come, she didn't even know how he was there so quickly, but he was. His slicker was gone; even his shoes were gone. And his arms were around her, helping her, lifting her up.

She choked, coughed, and assured him, "I'm all right. I—"

"Is your head okay? Seeing any spots?"

"No. No!"

She didn't have to climb to the rim again, he was lifting her over it, setting her feet into the tossing dinghy. He let her go because she was then below his reach. She quickly ducked to a sitting position to keep the dinghy from capsizing.

Then the sharp sound of a snap brought her staring back

up with horror; the line had broken, and the dinghy was instantly pitching away from the *Maggie Mae* with no lead, no purpose or reason.

Mike was still on deck.

Shouting at her, of all damned things.

"What?" she screamed against the fury of the wind. "Come on!"

Could he swim? she wondered, her heart pounding mercilessly. He was a sailor, wasn't he? But even if he could swim, the water was murderously rough! Currents were seething all around them. Breaking surface did not mean that one could breathe; the rain was like a blanket, cold and miserable. And there were the reefs below them, beautiful coral shelves that could be wickedly sharp and dangerous when the water was this strong, strong enough to toss a body about as if he were feather light. She knew how cruel those reefs could be. So beautiful yet so treacherous, waiting like sirens of time to prey upon the unwary, merciless even to those who knew and loved them.

"The oars, Mom!" Jason already had one; she was staring back at the *Maggie Mae* with open mouthed horror while her eight-year-old was maturely taking things in hand. "He said to get the oars!"

Nodding dumbly, she reached for the second oar and set it into the water. The initial force threatened to wrench her arm from her shoulder. How was Jason managing this?

And how could she be falling apart when she had her son to worry about?

But she looked back to the *Maggie Mae.* Taylor was no longer anywhere in sight. The deck looked bleak and naked. The sea seemed to stretch into countless yards between them, all frothing gray and vicious whitecaps.

"Oh, God!" she gasped out.

"He'll come!" Jason promised her. "He'll come!"

When? she wanted to shriek. Moments passed, endless moments, in which she saw nothing but the engulfing wrath of the waves, rising higher and higher. And she knew that below them, not far below them, the coral reached out in its deadly dance. The reefs were alive, with a combined will that beckoned, demanding its sacrifice. Long ago, pirates had likened the reefs to a seductress, one who lured boats to shipwreck, who reached out with eager, eerie fingers to claw at a man. . . .

"There he is!" Jason yelled out.

And he was, his head just breaking surface about ten yards away. Somehow, the sight of him steadied Katrina. She held her oar firm against the power of the water; she defied it with confidence. She couldn't row back to Mike's position, but with Jason's help she could keep the dinghy from drifting away.

He disappeared again; panic began to gnaw at her. But then a hand, large and bronzed and powerful, shot out of the water. Fingers found a hold on the dinghy.

Katrina dropped her oar into the boat and grasped his wrist with both hands. His head appeared again, and then his other hand. His steel gaze caught hers for just a second, and ludicrous as it was, he seemed to smile—amused by the anxiety he found in hers.

Then the muscles in his arms tightened and bulged, and he pitched his body into the dinghy.

For a moment he just lay there, legs crooked over one seat, torso bent. He gasped for breath and searched for her oar again. They still weren't home safe; they wouldn't be until they reached the beach. And even then there would be a quarter of a mile to go inland, through falling palms and branches, until they reached the house.

"You okay?" Jason shouted out.

That seemed to rouse Mike.

"Yeah, son, I'm fine." He gathered his length together carefully, not rising to rock the boat as he slid up to sit next to Katrina, reaching for her oar.

"I can do it—" she began.

"Not half as quickly," he told her, and for that she had no argument. She didn't have his strength.

The shore couldn't have been a hundred yards away, but it seemed that it took them an hour to get there. With every movement forward the wind pushed them back. The rain filled the dinghy until it seemed that it would sink with the weight.

But then they were there; the dinghy scraped the beach.

Katrina hopped out of it, grabbing the line. Jason was quickly at her side, and the two of them together grappled the towline. It dragged their weight, the tide ready to swallow it up again.

But then Mike was with them, adding his weight to theirs. Slowly, the dinghy crawled onto the shore. When it was deeply imbedded into the sand, he dropped the rope, the signal for Katrina and Jason to do the same.

For a moment they all fell to the sand—and gasped for breath. But the rain had not relented, and even as Katrina panted, willing her exhausted muscles to work again, there was a hand stretched to her.

Mike.

She took his hand and stumbled back to her feet. Jason, it seemed, was in control now. "Come on!" he called out.

Katrina was proud of him, very proud. He had met it all as a challenge, without complaint. He had to be freezing, clad only in his bathing trunks. And here he was like some adventurer, ready to forge ahead, already running into the trail . . .

"Stop him!" Katrina cried out with sudden horror. The palm fronds were touching the ground; she heard a horrendous snapping sound, and knew that somewhere, something larger and heavier than a palm had lost a branch.

Later, she would realize that there was one definite thing she had to appreciate about Mike Taylor. He could assess a situation quickly, without needing explanations.

He was after Jason, like a shot; he was standing above the boy when a whole bunch of coconuts fell like cannons.

Katrina screamed as the pair fell, and rushed to them. "Jason!"

Jason crawled out from beneath Mike's bulk, white and blanched with horror. "Mom!" For that instant he sounded like what he was—a very frightened little boy.

Katrina fell to her knees at Mike's side. Oh, Lord, what if he was unconscious, what if he was . . . *No!* She wouldn't think it!

"Captain Taylor!" She began to toss the coconuts a little madly away from him; then she heard him groan. His eyes opened, then shut instantly again as the rain lashed into them.

"Can you get up?" Katrina pleaded, pulling at his arms.

"Yeah, yeah," he said hoarsely, a frown furrowing his brow.

"Come on, please!" Katrina urged him to take his hands in her own. She didn't know if he was injured; she just knew that they had to find shelter, before something was uprooted completely and trapped them.

"I'm up, I'm up!" He gasped, and then he was standing, shaking his head slightly. He was wet to the bone, his shirt so thoroughly plastered to his body that he might as well have been bare chested. Katrina could see the sinews there, deep lines and grooves that clearly delineated a well-toned structure, and she felt somewhat better. He couldn't be really hurt; he appeared too powerful to be felled by any storm.

"Down the trail?" he asked suddenly.

Katrina nodded, and then she found that he had an arm around them each, that he was using his body again as a shelter for theirs. And she couldn't protest. She would have allowed anyone to serve as a shield for her son; he was her world. She would have laid her own body over him; Mike would never have let her, and it might well have been right. He had the size and the strength to protect them all.

It was as if the wind knew that they were escaping and was angered by the fact. It began to howl in keening banshee tones, ripping through the foliage with a newfound wrath. The fronds were flying and falling everywhere. Coconuts fell; Katrina screamed as a small mangrove was uprooted before them.

"The house!" Jason yelled out, and there it was, before them. Built on countless pilings, composed of solid concrete block and stucco and built to withstand the heartiest storm. Whitewashed and welcoming, it was just feet away.

But just then a palm came flying wickedly through the air; it caught Mike's shoulder and Katrina's midriff with such force that she cried out, doubling over.

"Run ahead!" Mike shouted to Jason, and Katrina found herself in his arms again, staring into his grim features as his hurried strides brought them along the tile path.

Jason pulled open the screen door; it flew off, the hinges breaking like straws. Balancing Katrina effortlessly, Mike reached for the hardier, wooden door, holding it with all his strength until they were inside, then pulling it shut before the wind could grasp it.

And then, just for a second, he stood there, silently surveying the house: the warm living room with its beige tones and oranges and Mexican tile flooring, the fireplace, the dining room with its immense Spanish oak table, the huge seascape on the wall, the softball and soccer trophies that lined the mantel, and the pictures that resided between them.

Then he looked down at Jason. "Where's your mother's bedroom?"

"I'm all right—" Katrina began, starting to struggle from his hold. But she wasn't. She was water-logged and frozen and miserable, and her middle hurt as if there were knives in it.

"This way," Jason said.

Shivering in misery, Katrina closed her eyes. She didn't want this man in her bedroom. Not because of him; because of her. Because she barely knew him, and she had made him part of a fantasy that should have belonged to James.

It was too easy to think of him as a man. Flesh and blood, muscle and tone and silver-and-steel eyes and a voice that was deep and husky, compelling . . .

Oh, God, what was wrong with her?

She opened her eyes and found herself lying on her bed. Ridiculously, she was glad that it was made, glad that the house was clean and neat, that her clothing was all picked up and away.

"We've got to get this thing off—" he was saying, and ridiculously, once again, she found herself grasping the soaked slicker and muttering, "No!"

She heard his vast sigh of impatience and felt like a stubborn two-year-old.

"Mrs. Denver, I am a physician, and if you've got broken ribs, we've got a problem to handle."

Then Jason was at her side, holding her hand, grinning down at her, both concerned and mischievous.

"Come on, Mom, behave! Maybe he'll even give you a balloon or a lollipop after the examination."

She turned crimson and shot her son a quick, warning glare. But he was laughing, and Mike was laughing, and suddenly, it seemed good just to hear them laugh.

She sat up and let them both pull away her slicker, and then the white terry robe she had snatched from Taylor's cabin floor.

"Now, that's it!" she protested, but Mike was way ahead of her, smooth and calm and cool.

"It should suffice—for now."

She felt his hands, grazing just beneath her breast, gentle, so very gentle. Large hands, long, tapering fingers, moving with care, touching her to the soul. Sliding along her rib-cage, so thoroughly, so lightly that they didn't even hurt her bruised flesh.

He grinned. "I can't find any breaks or cracks." He shrugged. "But be a little careful, huh?"

Katrina, seeing his eyes, feeling his eyes, just nodded. But then she murmured, "I've got to have a shower; the water lines will probably go with the storm and—"

"No shower. A careful bath." He looked at Jason. "Will you pour your mother a bath, Jason? Then take a shower yourself, and fill the tub and—"

"I know, I know!" Jason interrupted good-naturedly. "We get lots of storm warnings here, sir. We're all prepared for a hurricane. This is a hurricane isn't it?"

"Feels like it," Mike agreed. "I'll see what I can get on the

TV or radio as soon as I get the shutters down. Okay, Jason? Let's get started."

He was up, moving toward the door. Jason was heading toward her bathroom. She felt outnumbered, as if the men had decided that the fragile little woman was out of the way and they could get on with things!

She wasn't fond of the feeling. She had fought alone for far too long to be shoved aside.

But Mike had been there when she needed him—really needed him. When Jason had been threatened. He had protected him, risking his own life to do so.

"Captain Taylor!" she snapped out, and he turned.

"What"—she paused, absurdly having to moisten her lips to finish—"what about you? Are you all right? All the coconuts . . . ?

Mike chuckled lightly, and then he was afraid that the sound would catch in his throat, as his breath suddenly seemed to be doing. She was a mess—soaked and dirty, with all her glorious hair in wild wet strands—but she was a beautiful mess. No makeup, nothing; just the purity of her delicate structure. And he knew things, things she couldn't know . . . hadn't even guessed yet. And it made him feel as if he had known her all his life. Her temper, her pride . . . her sensuality. Even her desires, and her sorrows, the depth of her vulnerability, so hidden by determination.

She's just waiting for a chance to sue you and hang you, sailor! He mocked himself. But it didn't matter; not then. Her eyes were luminous and aqua as they rested on him with concern.

"I'm okay."

"You shouldn't go out again. We might not need the shutters."

"I think we're going to—it's a damned good thing you have them. And good ones. It won't take me a minute."

"But your head—your shoulders—"

"Hey, I'm all right. And I'm the physician, remember?"

He turned quickly to leave then, groaning inwardly, a little desperately. He clenched his jaw together, wishing once again with a great fervor that he could throttle whoever the hell it was who had messed up this project so damned badly.

Mike gave himself a shake and started for the door, listening to the wind. It should cleanse him; it should give him strength.

It didn't. As he moved around the house, bracing himself, bringing down the storm shutters, he felt torn and buffeted, in a far more vicious way than the elements could ever have done.

He enjoyed people; he liked women. He'd had lots of affairs over the years. But he'd never wanted to—to be touched again. Touched inside, at the soul, at the heart.

Somehow she—the woman who wanted to sue him and hang him—was reaching him. With more than her fingers. With more than the wild and passionate caress of which she had no memory. . . .

He paused, in his work, staring at the rain. "Physician!" he muttered savagely, "heal thyself!"

CHAPTER FOUR

Mike came back into the house; for a moment he stood dripping in the doorway, trying to catch his breath. Then he gave himself a shake. He needed a radio, or something.

"Want to take a shower?"

He blinked the water from his eyes and smiled at the boy who had come to stand curiously before him, dry and comfortable in a T-shirt and jeans. He was a nice kid, Mike decided. Bright and eager, friendly and easygoing. He was tall, very tall, considering his mother's size. His father must have been a tall man, Mike concluded, and then he was surprised that the thought gave him a little pang of something like envy.

"We've still got hot water," Jason offered.

Mike looked down at his sodden clothes. "Yeah, I suppose that I should. But first—have you got a radio?"

"Sure."

Jason led Mike through to the kitchen, a large room with an island range in the middle, and four wicker stools arranged about the extending counter that gave way into a family room.

Jason handed Mike a small transistor radio from the end of the counter. Mike began to fiddle with the switch, trying to home in on weather information.

"It is a hurricane," Jason said happily.

"Oh, yeah?" So far, all that Mike had found was a rock station, a gospel sermon, and a Spanish opera.

"Yep. Her name is Kathleen."

Mike frowned, staring up at Jason. "Kathleen?"

"Sure. She formed right over Cuba, whipped up in a sudden fury, and changed from a tropical storm to a hurricane at twelve noon. Highest sustained winds are one hundred miles an hour."

Mike frowned as he continued to play with the radio. "Where'd you hear that?"

"On the television, of course!"

The television. Here he was, sitting with a little battery-powered radio, grasping for anything, and the damn television was still working. Mike felt like a complete ass. He'd just assumed that the power would be shot!

He slid off the stool. "Jason, where's the television?"

"Back here," Jason said helpfully. "In the family room."

Jason led him to the rear of the room and switched on the television. Mike was able to discern that the storm was sitting stationary—moving very, very little—just east southeast of the Florida mainland. The eye was just barely east southeast of them right at the moment.

Then the power did blow.

"Well, back to the radio, I guess," Mike murmured with a sheepish grin. He ruffled Jason's hair. "At least we know what we've got, though."

"Yeah, sure," Jason agreed. "It's a real problem, though. The islands are going to be hurt badly."

"Umm?" Mike murmured, finding a weather report at last, but one in Spanish. His knowledge of the language was sketchy, and the commentator was speaking too quickly for Mike to understand him.

"People didn't have time to evacuate. And some of the islands flooded completely. Some of the houses are nothing but shacks. The National Guard has been out, but they can barely move."

"Did you hear that on the television too?" Mike asked absently, shaking the radio slightly to see if he couldn't hear through a barrage of static.

"Oh, no. I was talking to Pete Kenney, over in Islamorada. He's my best friend."

Once again Mike set the radio down, feeling like a fool. "Jason, did you talk to Pete on the phone?"

"Well, of course," Jason said matter-of-factly. Then he grinned. "It's way too wet for smoke signals, sir."

"Cute, kid, cute," Mike murmured, but his own sheepish grin softened the words.

"I take it you'd like to use the phone."

"Yeah, I sure would."

"Right at the end of the counter."

It was a French Provincial phone, white and gold, and it sat well with the old-fashioned atmosphere of the otherwise contemporary kitchen.

And it worked. To Mike's amazement he immediately reached an operator, and in less than a minute was connected with the base in Key West. Even more startling, he was able to reach a friend with access to the project, Lieutenant Commander Stan Thorpe.

"Damnation! but it's good to hear your voice, Mike! Stinking storm blew up so suddenly. First time I've ever heard of one whirling up so fast right here! We were desperate when we couldn't reach you—thought you'd been blown over or something! Where are you? There's nothing that can fly or take to the seas in this. Where did you find a working phone? The brass are worried to death about the civilian involvement. The woman and the boy. They all right?"

"Yeah, everyone is okay. I'm at their house on Rock Cay."

"You battened down? These things are real, real treacherous on those islands."

"Everything's good. Someone with some sense built this place with this kind of weather in mind. We're fairly well set."

Stan paused. "What about the project?"

"Oh, I could still do some testing. Diluted, maybe, but important, still. But I'm sure she'll raise a stink."

"The woman?"

"She's going to sue me, the U.S., the Navy—and anyone else she can get her hands on."

Stan started chuckling. "Don't worry! The admiral will talk to her and have her singing 'God Bless America' before you know it! What was she doing there, though?"

"She's says the Navy called and canceled."

"What? That's impossible!"

"I know, I know." He closed his eyes. He hadn't wanted a damned inhabited island to begin with. But they'd searched and searched—and Katrina Denver's island had offered the only ecological balance conducive to the testing he needed. 44DFS was a damned good thing—Michael knew it! It could save millions of lives as a defense weapon, it just had these side effects. And not until he studied the drug thoroughly, in the open as well as inside a laboratory, could he perfect it.

Damn her! he thought again. She'd been willing to take the government's money. But then she'd stayed—and she was blaming him!

"Stan, when do you think the admiral will get here?"

"Soon as the skies clear, Mike. He's here, bunked out in his office. Want me to wake him?"

"No, there's nothing he can do now, I don't suppose. The storm is just sitting still?"

"She's moving at three miles an hour, can you beat that? The bridge is already out down here. They've got Guardsmen moving around in tanks where they can to reach the shore people. This has been one hell of a bitch—no warning."

"Yeah, well, I guess we can't control the weather yet."

"There's something else you might have trouble controlling, Mike," Stan said softly—as if he didn't want to be overheard.

"What's that?"

"Stradford. He's on your case. He's going to try to use this to kill the 44DFS project before you can get it off the ground. He's already got clearance to show up with the admiral. You know the old boy—he's all for supporting you, but he believes in listening to the opposition too."

Mike leaned an elbow against the counter, ran his free set of fingers through his hair, and sighed. Albert Stradford was a fool, and a dangerous man. He didn't believe in any weapon that didn't kill or maim. They shared rank and they shared degrees, and they had been at odds forever.

And fate was a frivolous thing, continually tossing the two of them together.

"I'll watch out for Stradford," Mike said brusquely.

"Yeah, well," Stan said a little bit huskily, "at the moment I'm just glad to hear you're alive. And you've got some time. Unless Kathleen picks up some speed, it will be a couple of days before we can get anything moved."

Static was starting to form on the line. Mike didn't think that the phone would last much longer.

"Good. And thanks for the warning, Stan. Oh, do me one favor; give Toni a call for me, will you? I'm sure she's heard about the storm, and that she's worried."

"Will do."

Stan broke the connection, but the phone died right then, before Mike could replace the receiver.

It was several seconds after Mike hung up that he realized Jason was still sitting at the end of the counter, watching him. Little prickles of uneasiness ran through Mike as he wondered what the boy had heard.

Jason gave him a wry, apologetic smile. "She really won't sue you."

Mike grimaced and wandered into the kitchen. "You don't think so, huh?"

"Naw—she's a lot of growl. No real bite."

"Oh, yeah?" Mike couldn't help but grin at the revelation. "Got anything to drink in here?"

"Want a cold beer?"

"Sure."

Jason skimmied down from his chair and opened the refrigerator; Mike noticed that it was as neatly arranged as the house. He accepted the beer with a nod of thanks and devoured it, only aware then of just how dry his throat had been.

"Who's Toni?" Jason asked suddenly, almost causing Mike to choke on a swallow.

"My daughter."

"Daughter? You're married?" Jason said with obvious dismay.

Mike shook his head. "I—uh—lost my wife."

"And you can't find her?"

There was something so earnest about the question that Mike had to smile, albeit a bit sadly.

"She died, Jason."

"Like my dad," he stated flatly, bowing his head. Then he looked up cheerfully. "Want to see him?"

"Your dad? Sure."

Jason was out of the kitchen and into the living room, reaching up to the mantel to procure one of the pictures.

"They say I look like him," Jason said proudly.

Mike gazed at the picture. It was of a young man, lean and lanky like his son. He was nice looking, and even in the photo it was clear that he had the same enthusiasm for life as his son.

"You do look like him," Mike said.

Jason took the picture back, deep in thought. Then he looked at Mike peculiarly. "I don't remember him. Don't tell my mom. I was only three when he died." He paused. "But he was a hero, a real live one. He died out on the reefs. Some dumb kids were out—old kids, you know, teenagers—with bad diving equipment. Dad dragged the girl in; he had to go back 'cause the boy got his foot stuck in some coral. He got the boy free, but something happened to him. I don't know, a wave or something. His head was all cut up when Mom found him."

"Your mother—found him?"

"Yeah. He was dead when she reached him."

"But you don't remember any of it?"

"No, I heard about it all. Mom doesn't talk about it, just to remind me how dangerous the reefs can be. But my friends know things from their parents. They say that she tried everything to bring him back. She's a water safety instructor, you know. She's got all kinds of certificates. But"—he shrugged—"nothing worked on Dad. She kept at it for hours; the doctor who came from Islamorada finally had to pull her away and sedate her."

Mike touched Jason's hair. "I'm sorry, son. It sounds like he was a real great man. A hero."

Jason set the portrait back on the mantel. "We've got to do something about you before she gets out of the bathtub."

"Pardon?"

"You've been dripping everywhere. I'll get some paper towels. You go take a shower."

Jason took off for the kitchen to get the paper towels. Mike had to grin; it had been a long time since he had been in conspiracy with an eight-year-old to save his hide from a chewing out.

But a hot shower would feel damned good right now. He felt chilled to the bone.

He followed Jason to the kitchen. "Can I borrow your shower?"

"Yeah, sure, but you don't need to. There's a guest bedroom all set up next to my mother's. There's towels, soap, even extra toothbrushes. And there should have been enough water left in the heater for it to be warm."

Mike smiled gratefully and headed toward the guest bedroom. When he found it, he instinctively tried to switch on the bedroom light. The gloomy darkness remained, and he remembered that the power was shot.

He looked around curiously. It was a warm room with a queen-sized bed in the center, an armoire, an old-fashioned mirrored dresser with a washbowl and ewer in an early-American blue-and-white floral pattern. Bookcases flanked the bed; there was an afghaned recliner by the window.

He passed through the room and into the ultramodern bath. The tub was spacious and deep, "Roman" style, in gold-threaded pink marble; there was a matching sink and dark-crimson curtains to complete the picture.

Mike quickly shed his clothing and even more quickly adjusted the water; he knew that the leftover hot water in the tanks couldn't last long. As soon as it turned cold on him, he stepped out of the tub and grabbed one of the immense white-and-gold towels off the rack. He vigorously dried his face, then paused, realizing that he hadn't anything to put back on. Grimacing, he wrapped the towel around his lower torso—thankful that it was such a large one—and decided that Jason might be able to help him find something to wear.

He started down the hallway. It had gotten so dark that he could barely see. At the edge of the living room he paused. Candles were burning on the coffee table.

There were voices coming from the kitchen.

"—that's crazy, Mom! We were supposed to have been gone!"

"Jason, they canceled! Someone called and—"

"But, Mom—"

Mike grimaced; obviously Jason had taken his words on the phone to heart; he was trying to talk his mother out of legal action.

"If you'd give him half a chance, you'd like him too!"

"I don't dislike him." This was spoken crisply, very crisply.

"Then quit being such a—witch!"

"Jason!"

It was time for him to step in, Mike decided. He'd enjoyed his young champion, but he didn't want family dissension between them over him, not on top of everything else.

Yet he hesitated, confused by the flash of raw emotion that flashed through him.

I like you, too, Jason, he thought. *I love Toni more than anything on earth, and I never knew that I was missing anything, but I guess I would have liked a son: someone just like you, eager and adventurous, so open to life.*

His thoughts switched from the boy to the mother, and he shuddered with a sizzle of sudden, red-hot heat. How could he want her so badly, so completely? With such yearning, such fascination? They'd just barely met.

No, he'd held her: in fantasy, in reality. He had held her, known her, touched her, loved her, and he could not forget. He knew the shape and form and substance of her like the back of his hand. They'd fought the wind together; he was certain he'd even touched her soul despite the walls of steel around it.

He gave himself a shake. Let it lie! He warned himself firmly. In time he'd be gone. She would slip back into her private world, unaware that it had ever been shattered. And he could go back to his own escape: work, his dream that he could change things, that what had happened to Margo might never, never come to pass again. Oh, it was idealistic, yes; it would never come in his lifetime. But what else had he left but the vision, the dream, the prayer that it could all be changed?

Katrina's just a woman, he told himself, and stepped into the kitchen.

Katrina, sorting out silverware and about to snap at Jason, looked up. She had not heard him approaching, but nevertheless she had been aware that he was there. He was a presence, eclipsing everything else around her.

He was there, all right: standing in front of her in nothing but a towel. Stupidly, she just stared at him for a minute. He was nicely built, well muscled, tanned, possessing a thickly, golden-haired chest. He looked like a fighter, with a flat stomach and perfectly tapered waist.

His eyes caught hers; she realized that she had been staring, and she flushed furiously, then lashed out to cover her embarrassment.

"Captain Taylor, what the hell do you think you're doing?"

"Mrs. Denver," he said smoothly, inclining his head toward her a bit, "I'm quite sorry if I've—startled you. But I'm afraid I simply forgot to grab a change of clothing for the evening."

She flushed again at the insinuative sound of his voice.

"Give him something of Dad's," Jason suggested.

"Don't be ridiculous; your father's things would never fit him," Katrina murmured.

"What about a robe?"

"Umm, I suppose," she muttered, now watching the man

in her kitchen with a hardened jaw and wary eyes. She set the silver down, warned Jason to watch the soup bubbling on the Sterno fire, and picked up one of the candles she had burning on the counter.

"Come on," she told Mike briefly, walking past him. "I'll find . . . something to lend you."

"That's very generous," Mike murmured sarcastically.

"Anything is better than you walking around half nude," she sweetly retorted.

"Why? Do I excite you too much?"

She stopped dead in her tracks, then flung around so quickly that she almost burned him with the candle.

"Hardly, Captain. Uniforms—or the lack of them—never did excite me much."

Mike just smiled, with a cryptic look in his eyes that made her want to hit him at the same time it made her feel as if she was melting into a pool of rippling heat.

Once again she turned, throwing open the door to her own room, setting the candle on her dresser, and burrowing through the left set of drawers.

"It's going to have to be a robe," she muttered. "James was a very slender man."

Mike crossed his arms over his chest and leaned against the door frame, watching her with a curious frown. The entire left set of drawers was still filled with her husband's clothing.

"You've kept all your husband's things, Mrs. Denver?"

"I—uh—haven't had time, I guess, to clear them out."

"Five years, and you haven't had time."

"Oh, shut up! Who asked your opinion? You're lucky, Captain Taylor, that you're in the house at all. After what you did, I should leave you out in the damn storm."

"Oh, I don't think that I'd stay there."

"Forcing your way in would be illegal."

"You're suing me anyway, what difference would a few more offenses make?"

"Here!"

She tossed something at him; it was a robe, much like the

one she had borrowed from him on the boat, but velvet instead of terry.

"Thanks," he said softly.

She was just sitting on the bed. In the candlelight her eyes had a strange luster.

"I'm sorry that I have to touch your husband's things."

He was—and then he wasn't. Someone needed to wake her up.

She shook her head briskly. "He never wore that, Captain, so it doesn't matter in the least."

Something about the cool tone of her voice irritated him all the more. "Well, like I said, thanks. I'll be real careful not to let the slit fall too far open, knowing the effect naked flesh seems to have on you."

"Oh!" she exclaimed, and looked at him, as if realizing just how naked he would be beneath the robe.

She started digging through the drawers again.

Amused and somewhat confused, Mike grinned. "His pants couldn't possibly fit me."

She produced a pair of snow-white briefs and tossed them to him. He held them, eying her inquiringly.

"They'll fit?"

"Oh, do get out of my way!" she snapped, rushing past him. "Fruit of the Looms fit anyone!"

He couldn't help laughing as he watched her hurry back toward the kitchen. But then his laughter faded, and he was sober again. He'd felt that he'd violated her; that he'd had no right. He could keep her innocent of it—and he had no idea if it would be the only right thing to do, or the crime of the century.

He didn't look much better in the robe, Katrina decided; it was probably because he'd looked so damned good in the towel. He was barefoot and casual, and she realized once again, as she served Sterno-heated soup, salad, and fried steaks at the kitchen counter, that what bothered her most about him was the simple fact that he was so very male. He was male in the sound of his voice, in his laughter, in his stance, in the way that he looked at her, in the way that he filled the air around her.

"That's plenty, thanks!"

She paused, staring at the man in her thoughts. She might have been feeding a dozen rabbits, she'd put so much salad on his plate. But she wasn't about to admit that her mind had been wandering around him.

"Are you sure?" she asked politely.

"Yeah, quite sure. But thanks very much."

"Boy, I'm sure glad she did that to your plate and not mine!" Jason said. "I'd have to eat it all. You're a guest; if you can't scarf it all down, you don't have to."

"Jason!"

He stared down at his food and offered a contrite "Sorry, Mom." But Mike could see the smile that played about his lips, and he had to glance down to hide his own smile.

Katrina ignored them both and sat next to Jason rather than Mike. "He's not really a guest," she told Jason, staring at Mike over her son's head. "He's kind of a refugee, a waif from the storm."

"Or a forcible foe, Mrs. Denver?"

"Her first name is Katrina," Jason piped up.

"I know."

"Do you think that she's cute?"

"Very."

"Jason, you can pack yourself off to bed this instant!"

"Yes, ma'am!" Jason agreed convivially, too convivially. Katrina realized too late that her eight-year-old was in the middle of matchmaking and that she had fallen straight into his trap.

She felt a little numb as he humbly kissed her cheek. "Night, Mom." He offered Mike a hand. "Good night, Captain Taylor."

"I've got a first name, too, Jason. It's Mike, and you're welcome to use it."

Jason grinned in a way that tugged at Katrina's heart. She realized how much he had missed male companionship.

Sorry, son! she thought, watching his slim back disappear

from the kitchen. *This just isn't it! I'm not at all sure what I'm doing with this man in my house except that I can't throw him out into a storm.*

But I couldn't even if I wanted to, she thought wryly. *I couldn't budge him an inch in a direction in which he didn't want to go!*

She looked up suddenly, sensing Mike's eyes on her. But when her gaze met his, he rose, picking up his dish.

"We've still got running water?"

"*Ah*—Cold, yes. But listen, I can pick up—"

"You made the meal," he said lightly. "Quite a good one, especially under the circumstances. Not many refugees eat this well."

"Captain Taylor—" She started to rise with her dishes; he caught her wrists against the counter.

"I'm a good dishwasher, and you're anxious to go tell your son good-night again, because you snapped at him. Go do it."

"I did not snap at him. His behavior was atrocious."

"He's a hell of a good kid and you know it; he's wise beyond his years. Kids who lose a parent tend to be that way, Katrina. Soften up! Go to him; it's what you want to do."

She shot him a belligerent stare, more than ready to argue again for the sake of argument, except that he was right. Jason was behaving badly, but she should have understood and shrugged it off. Yet she couldn't, because Mike had been on her mind, somehow touching her too deeply. She didn't want to remember what it was like to want someone and be wanted in return, to laugh and flirt, because love was something that hurt.

Without another word she left the kitchen and headed for Jason's bedroom. He was already in pajamas; she could smell Crest on his breath.

She hugged him, and he hugged her back, tightly. "I love you," he whispered.

"I love you too. More than anything in the world."

"You're special, Mom."

"You are too, Jase."

"So's he."

"Oh, Jason—"

"No. I'm serious. And you—you never date, Mom."

"I just haven't met anyone I want to date, Jason."

"But he could be different."

"Jason, he might be married, for all I know."

"He's not."

"How do you know?"

"I asked him."

"Oh, Jason!" She stared into his eyes; they were like James's eyes, dark and sincere and sensitive. "I realize that you want a father, honey, but you can't go picking out a guy in one day! And I have a definite, and very important, bone to pick with this particular man! We could have been hurt—"

"But we weren't! Be a little nice to him, okay?"

Katrina sighed. There really wasn't any way to win an argument with a determined eight-year-old. She kissed him on the forehead and stood up. "Night, son."

"Love you."

"Love you."

She left him, thinking that Mike was right; Jason was old for his age. That fact made her proud, but it also hurt her a little.

She entered the meagerly lit kitchen. Mike wasn't there.

"Pssst!"

Katrina turned around. He was sitting on the sofa. He'd made coffee for them both and brought it out to the living room, where a few candles burned, very intimately.

He smiled—a bit devilishly, she thought. His eyes were truly silver in the night, in the candle glow. He patted the spot on the couch beside him. "Mrs. Denver?"

Enter the lion's den!

She wasn't afraid of him. She was, however, very afraid of herself, of her thoughts, of her feelings. He'd brought his strange potions to her island, and her chemistry hadn't been at all the same since.

And the problem was, she wasn't under the influence of any drug anymore.

CHAPTER FIVE

"I want to hear about this phone call," Mike told Katrina, watching her stir cream into her coffee. "Or rather, start at the beginning for me. You agreed to rent out the island, right?"

He wasn't touching her, and it certainly didn't seem as if he intended to, either. His leg was slightly hiked as he sat, his back to the curve of the couch. He sipped his coffee, that was it.

"Yes, I agreed. They said they were working on experimental exercises." She paused, reflecting dryly. "I thought they wanted to crawl through the foliage or something. Anyway, I received the papers, I showed them to my attorney, he said they were fine, and he returned them for me. Then I got a call from a man named Admiral Riker—"

"Riker?"

"Yes, I'm positive—"

"There is no Admiral Riker; not that I know of. It must have been a prank that someone played on you."

"But no one knew! I told my parents I was just going over to Islamorada for relaxation. That's the same story I told everyone!"

He stared at her, exasperated. "You just accepted a phone call that it was off and that was it."

"Well, yes, he was official—"

"He wasn't official!"

"Then it's the damned Navy's fault, not mine!"

He frowned. "So, the Navy will get to the bottom of it, I promise you. But what about you?"

"What do you mean?"

"Are you going to sue?"

"I—I don't know," she faltered. "Maybe if you told me more about this project."

He stared at her a long, long time. "All right. But it is highly classified information."

"You'll trust me?" she asked dryly.

"I plan on asking you to trust me."

She inhaled sharply, watching his eyes. "Go on."

He sipped his coffee, returning her stare so intensely she grew even more confused.

"I'm working on a gas that's a defensive weapon. It can counter a number of chemical and germ weapons, keep them from harming and killing people. It has a side effect, though—"

"Dreams?" Katrina swallowed and asked.

"Yes. Physically, it doesn't do any harm. But—well, it's similar to mind control, which, if used improperly, could be horribly insidious. And this island is a rare biological wonder. Endless small creatures. I intended to study the duration of the drug on animals—"

"Such as humans?" Katrina interrupted tartly, despite herself.

He gazed at her patiently.

"We've calculated," he said, "that the effect on large animals wears off in forty-eight hours maximum. On smaller creatures it ranges from three days to a week."

"And you got a chance to study us!" she exclaimed.

His profile, highlighted by the candles, looked strong and rugged and very proud, and, at this moment, a little haggard.

"I didn't study you," he said huskily.

"Why not? You're a scientist, aren't you? When opportunity knocks . . . Besides—you did study us. You had television cameras going all night."

"Those were to make sure that you were all right."

She didn't want to go any farther; she was suddenly afraid to ask him what had come of his observations.

"So—so what now?"

"What now?" He finished his coffee and set his cup down, then lifted his hands and looked at her with a grimace. "We're in the middle of a hurricane. It's howling all around us. Rain is pouring down in sheets. That's what's now."

Something about his wry look caused her to smile. "I realize we're in the middle of a hurricane. But it will end by tomorrow night, or the day after." She hesitated. "Will you still be able to accomplish anything?"

"Probably. One important thing will be to salvage what I can off the *Maggie Mae.* If she isn't completely broken to bits."

"Still, how could you use a deadly drug—"

"It isn't a deadly drug!" he thundered.

Katrina was on her feet, moving agitatedly toward the shuttered window. The government had been careless; it deserved her wrath!

And then again, no real harm had come to them. And maybe this thing was some real benefit to science; she didn't understand it, but she felt that she understood Michael Taylor, his character, his soul. And if he proclaimed with such vehemence that it wasn't a deadly drug, then surely . . .

But why? Why was she giving in so easily? He'd been gentle; he'd also taunted her and teased her. And the night she'd spent aboard his yacht held a mystery that haunted her mind, which would not come clear.

Did she want it to come clear?

She was embarrassed; she was fascinated. But she also had to admit that she didn't really want him to go away. She didn't know what she felt or wanted at all. He was a very definite sexual threat, and she didn't know if she wanted to run, or, after all this time alone, go for that challenge.

He watched her, watched all the conflicting emotions cross her face, and his only thought was that he wanted to go to her, hold her, and swear that by his life he meant no harm; that he would fight man or beast for her, that—he had fallen a little bit in love. Maybe a lot in love. It had begun in a cloud of wafting fog, but the seeds had been real. Her whispers, her fingers pressing against him, the fervor of her kiss and the rhythm of her form . . . all had invaded him. *So tell her!* he commanded himself.

I can't!

You have to!

I will. Just—not now. Soon . . .

He was standing very near her. She could feel the warmth of his breath against her neck, the vitality that seemed to wind around her like a caress of strength and assurance.

He was touching her then; his hands were on her shoulders, swirling her around to face him. And his eyes were tense in the candlelight; they gleamed with color as deep as steel, as caring as soft silver.

"Couldn't you trust me?" he asked her. "Believe in me?"

"I barely know you."

"You know me very well."

She didn't know how well. She was suddenly very afraid; she wanted to run.

She backed away from him, her fists tightened at her sides.

"Oh, for heaven's sake! I'm not really going to do anything to you! Ask Jason—Mom is a sucker. I've never sued anyone in my life and I'm hardly likely to start with a wayward Navy doctor! Stay on the island, study whatever you can. Just don't you dare let any of that pink stuff of yours get near Jason or me again!"

And then she did run. Not literally. She managed to walk by him with a terse "Good night, Captain Taylor."

But she knew that she had run. And she thought that he knew it too.

It was a perfect night to sleep. The sound of the high winds was actually lulling. Katrina felt safe; she'd faced this kind of weather before.

The house, she knew, was secure, built with the best and heartiest shutters available. She and James had been young when they'd built it, but young and sensible. Everyone had thought them crazy to live on the island, but Katrina and

James had seen their Eden, and they'd known damn well that they were perfectly sane. Her house, his house, their paradise. Strong, strong walls around them . . .

And you've never escaped those walls, have you? she asked herself, lying there, alone still, with the sounds of the night.

Walls, yes, that she had made. Because it had been so sudden and shocking and painful to be alone. Her marriage might have lasted only four years, but she and James had been together forever. Both native Conchs—or Key Westerners—they had grown up together, gone to all the same schools. In kindergarten he had pulled on her ponytails. In grade school they had tousled in mud puddles. By junior high he had carried her books, and by high school they had known they'd be married as soon as school was out.

She twisted in her bed, pressing her face against the pillow. James was dead. Had been, for almost five years. It had surely been one of the greatest injustices ever; he'd been only twenty-three, carefree and handsome, with his whole life ahead of him. And then he had been killed. And no matter how she had tried to breathe new life into him, she could not.

It had taken her a year to realize that he was really gone, that she wouldn't hear him whistling, coming into the house with a sly smile and a pack of Florida lobster alive and kicking in a net. A year, just to realize that no, he would not return. . . .

Then there were Ted and Nancy Denver, ravaged forever by the loss of their oldest son. How could she ever face them and say, *I'm going on a date?* They were such good people. . . .

And there was no one alive who could love her as James had. She was afraid of caring, of not being cared for in return. It was easier to grow walls of stone all around herself, to devote herself to Jason, and fight the world on his behalf. To be the "coral princess," cool, aloof, virginal—and independent.

Except that Mike Taylor had changed it all on her. Mike

and his marvelous dream machine. Pink clouds that eased away pain and made every fantasy real. Too real.

Katrina tossed again, staring up at the ceiling. Even in her dream she had known that James could not come back from the dead. The man in her dream had not been James. He had been very tall, broad, and muscled. His tender strength had been as steely as his eyes, sword steel, touched by silver magic.

But it was logical. She'd seen Taylor's eyes just before she'd lost her grip on reality. She had turned him into a lover; Jason had made him into a space conqueror. That, apparently, was what the pink fog did to one. . . .

Except that she had awakened blissfully bare.

Ah, that pink dream machine!

But life was not dreams; it was full of truths. Harsh, brutal truths. And the harsh, brutal truth was that she was aching tonight. She was alone, afraid, and confused and she was amazed and incredulous at the strange twists and pleas of her mind.

He was there. In her house. In the very next room. In a fantasy she could see herself rising, drifting to that room. Entering silently, standing above him until he opened his eyes.

Once in his arms, she wouldn't have to explain that she was rusty, that she was afraid that she couldn't possibly please him, that it was totally ludicrous and not in the least moral for her to be there, but . . .

She wanted him. To be held by him. Loved by him. Even if it was in a dream.

He was like James: tall, ready to laugh, eager to tease, the hint of a devil about him.

Yet he was nothing like James at all. He was much older, a little tougher, a little harder, a little more cynical. His was a handsome face, etched with the character of time, rugged from the sun and wind and the secrets in the heart. She wanted to know him.

Disloyal! What had her love for James been—that love

she had clung to so desperately!—if she was ready to crawl to a stranger?

She would never do it. Never in a thousand years. She would twist and toss with the wind, but she would never leave the security of her walls.

She didn't know that it was dawn before she fell asleep. She had no way of knowing, because the island remained under a dark pall.

"Boardwalk! Oh, no! You can't buy Boardwalk!" Jason was protesting dramatically when Katrina left her room the next morning.

Except that it wasn't morning, she noted distractedly, glancing at her watch. It was well after noon.

Jason and Mike were stretched out on the living room floor, playing Monopoly. Mike must have set his clothes to dry overnight, or at least his pants. He was bare chested and barefooted, but his own white trousers stretched over the length of his legs. Her heart began to beat a little erratically at the sight of his naked, hair-roughened chest. This irritated her. After all, she saw naked chests all the time. They were a dime a dozen in this water sport haven, where men seldom went swimming, fishing, or snorkeling in more than shorts.

But they did not have chests like his. . . .

He was propped up on one elbow. He turned to her, as if sensing she was standing there.

"Hey. Want to play? I don't think that Jason would mind starting over."

Katrina hooked her thumbs into her jeans pockets and shook her head. She averted her eyes from Mike's and looked at her pleasantly smiling son.

"Did you find something to eat?"

"Mike made pancakes."

She looked back to her uninvited guest. His eyes were enigmatic as he shrugged.

"We left you some."

"Thanks."

Stiffly, she walked on past them. They barely seemed to notice; she had hardly been an intrusion on their game.

The thought that Mike had gotten up in time to make breakfast for her son rankled her, especially since it had been his fault she had awakened so late. He'd confused her, he'd made her think all night long, think about things that she had put behind herself. . . .

He'd left more than pancakes. There was coffee, hot and steaming on the Sterno stove, and there was also a plate of crispy, delicious bacon.

What was she going to do with the day? she asked herself dryly as she munched on the bacon. Try to avoid both her son and Mike? Not a good plan. It was a large house, but it seemed very small, now that they were all confined in it.

She stopped chewing suddenly, aware that something was different, not at all sure of what it was.

And then she knew. The wind had stopped.

Katrina gulped down the rest of her coffee and hurried out to the living room. The front door was open. Mike was standing just outside of it; Jason was right behind him.

"Hey!" she called a little anxiously, running up behind her son, then passing him to give Mike a firm tap on the back. "What are you doing? This is probably just the eye—"

He turned around, looking down at her. "I know it's the eye. I'll be right back in. Take Jason and go back inside."

"What—?"

"Hurry, please. Dammit, will you do as I say?"

He was implacable and cold and his hands came to her shoulders like talons, firmly turning her around and shoving her toward the door.

"Mike—" she began, trying to wrench away. And then she broke off, because at the side of the house—right next to the concrete porch—there was a pair of squirrels. Cute little fluffy brown squirrels. Mating.

It was difficult to tell where one squirrel began and the other ended, so engrossed were they in one another. Squirrels were not usually passionate animals, but these squirrels were definitely passionate. She'd never seen creatures go at the act with such absolute abandon ever in her life.

"Man, are they going at it!" Jason laughed from the doorway.

"Oh!" Katrina gasped. "Jason, get back in the house! Now, this minute! I mean it!"

"Really, Mom, I'm almost nine! Don't make a federal case about a bunch of squirrels!"

Bunch of . . . ? She turned around. Mike, hands on his hips, eyes angry, was staring at her. And beyond her, the small clearing in front of her house was full of the creatures—all blindly enjoying the nature of their sexes.

"Captain Taylor!" she thundered. "You pervert! I'll have your—" She cut herself off just in time. "I'll—I'll—I will see that you're court-martialed for this! Drawn and quartered and hung out to wash!"

"Just go back inside," he told her rigidly.

She did, shoving Jason in before her. Then, in a high pitch of fury, she swung around and locked the bolt on the door.

"Mom, what are you doing?"

"He deserves to stay out there!" she snapped.

"Mom, come on, I'm old enough, I know that babies don't come from storks! If you're mad at him because of me—"

"I'm mad at him because he should be shot!"

"You can't leave him out in a storm!"

No, she couldn't. But she wanted to. She wanted to very badly. Why? Because the squirrels had embarrassed her?

No, dammit! Because she'd had a dose of the same damn stuff the squirrels had received! How the hell had she acted? She'd fallen asleep, passed out. But she'd awakened with her bathing suit on the floor next to the bunk and . . .

Blank. Dead end. She didn't want to know any more. All she wanted to do was wring his neck and—

"Katrina! Open the damned door!"

"Mom!"

Her back was to it, and she couldn't seem to force herself

to move. She felt frozen, in time, in eternity. She had to keep him out. If he got back through the door again—

"Dammit! I'm not about to while away the hours of a hurricane with a bunch of palm trees."

She didn't move, but suddenly the door did. His fist slammed against it and the wood reverberated, cracking. She swallowed, miserably aware that he had the raw strength to break it down; she'd be left without a door—and with a very irate man on her hands.

"Stop it!" she shrilled out, and motioned for Jason to open the door.

When he opened it, Katrina noticed that the wind was already picking up again—from the opposite direction. It was definitely only the eye that had passed them.

Mike caught the open door before it could be swept by the wind; he closed it, bolted it, then leaned against it, staring at her as if she were a snake.

"That was stupid. Utterly stupid—and lethal!" he told her, heedless of Jason, the words bitten off and hoarse as he spoke them.

She retaliated with the only words that came to her mind.

"Squirrel murderer! Those poor creatures! Now they'll be caught in all that wind and rain because of your stupid little pink drug! They'll die without the sense to seek shelter!"

He left the door and stalked toward her. Instinctively, she backed away.

"They'll find shelter now. They haven't become blind or dumb! But you! You'd kill a man over your own sick little hang-ups?"

"Sick hang-ups! You son of a bitch! What—"

"Hey! Wait, guys, please!" Jason suddenly begged, reminding them both that he was there. "I'm a kid, remember? Grown-ups just hate to act like kids themselves in front of real ones, don't they?"

Katrina stared at her son, wishing for a moment that she could paddle his too-grown-up rear, then realizing that he was very, very right, and that even if she had been upset about the squirrels, she should have never done anything so childish and dangerous as locking Mike out.

And Jason was trying so hard. . . .

She stared back at Mike. He was still tensed and rigid. His fingers were wound into fists that twitched as if they longed to move—for her throat? Or just for her arms, to shake her thoroughly? The muscles in his shoulders and chest were knotted with strain.

He closed his eyes and swallowed. His fingers tightened again, then relaxed, and he swung around with a shrug.

"Sorry, Jason. I really am," he said. "Where were we? Ah, yes—I was just about to buy Park Place."

"Hey—aren't you supposed to be nice and let me win?"

"Not on your life, son. If you play the game, you've got to be willing to get beaten!"

Willing to get beaten . . .

Katrina was not. She turned and fled back to her own room, in full retreat.

She came back out again, several hours later. She wasn't about to let Mr. Too-Perfect-Taylor fix dinner.

She didn't really trust much of what was left in the refrigerator, so she decided on grilled cheese sandwiches, Campbell's soup, and fruit salads—canned peaches and pineapples on beds of lettuce, with a decorative cherry set on top.

She didn't call Mike and Jason until she was ready for them, with the counter all neatly set. And when she did call them, Jason suddenly decided that he had to go to his own room to wash his hands.

Mike came in alone. They watched one another warily, like a pair of fencers taking their mark.

He went straight for the freezer, reached in, and found a can of beer. "Want one?" he asked her coolly.

"I didn't know that I had beer in the freezer," she replied.

"I switched them—yesterday. The freezer retains more cold."

"Umm. Except that this is my house. I don't remember offering you the beer."

He blinked, but displayed no emotion. "If you begrudge the beer, the food, the sleeping quarters, anything, I can only promise that you'll be reimbursed."

"Is that it, Captain Taylor? Reimburse people, and they'll just accept anything that way?"

"You want a beer or not?" He flipped the snap on the beer can; she heard the rush of air. But he barely extended it toward her.

"Yes, thank you, I *will* take one of my *own* beers!"

And she did, stepping toward him to snatch it away with such a vengeance that the beer sprayed out, yellow and foamy, all over his chest. And standing there, she was a little horrified and awed by her own act, and more than a little contrite, a state of mind nurtured by the silver wrath that seemed to touch her like a blaze from the depths of his eyes.

"Oh!" she murmured, dismayed. "Sorry . . ."

A little blindly she reached for one of the dinner napkins and made tentative sopping motions on his chest. And she felt his bare flesh, hot like fire, smooth and sleek. She was very close, and suddenly she was looking up into his eyes.

She trembled, horribly aware that there was something there, something in the way that he looked at her, something in the way that he could make her feel. It was as if he could see her naked, as if he could put his arms around her, and she would come, fitting nicely, because she had been there before. It wasn't a leer. It was just a look that knew . . . and though it bore remnants of anger, it also bore tenderness, and something so intimately sexual that she might have sworn she had known him a long, long time; that they had been both friends and lovers for ages. . . .

"Your hair," he murmured, and he touched her, lifting her hair over her shoulder, smoothing it down her back, his eyes holding hers all the while. "The beer . . . you were getting beer on it."

And he was getting his fingers tangled into it. It was a web of silk, of seduction.

"It's—it's good for hair, I hear," Katrina heard herself mumble. "I have to wash it anyway." She blinked and backed away. It was the only way to break the spell.

Jason walked into the room while Mike was still drying himself off. "Looks great. I love grilled cheese," Jason said. "Too bad we don't have hurricanes more often."

"Don't say that," Katrina told him. "This storm is going to devastate a lot of people. The damage to docks and boats and homes and maybe even roads is going to be horrible."

"I know." Jason sighed. "I don't want that to happen—I just like grilled cheese."

"I rather like them myself," Mike said. He handed Katrina a fresh can of beer. Their eyes met just briefly before they both took their separate seats on either side of Jason.

And dinner went nicely. Jason talked about how much fun it was to come and go from school by boat; Mike told him a little about the ships on which he had served.

It was during that conversation that she learned that the *Maggie Mae* hadn't been a military vessel, that she had been his own.

"Gee, what a shame!" Jason said to him. "Man, it's too bad she got all wrecked."

Mike shrugged. "The *Maggie Mae* can be replaced. Human life can't. We all got off safely, which is what counts."

Katrina played with them that night—a rousing game of "Hungry, Hungry Hippos." She was amazed that the rather silly game didn't seem to bother Mike in the least. Somehow, it was hard to imagine that the same man who commanded ships and spent hours in a laboratory could stretch out on a floor and enjoy trying to capture little balls in the mouth of a plastic hippopotamus.

She was somewhat nervous—and somewhat relieved—when Jason yawned and announced that he was going to bed. Even if there was something resembling a truce between herself and Mike, she meant to talk to him.

She kissed and hugged Jason, who then said good-night to Mike with a handshake and a look that seemed to hold a secret meaning. Katrina ignored it. She waited until Jason's door was closed, until she was quite certain that he was in bed and drifting off, before she started to talk.

He was standing near the mantel. She was still on the floor, stretched out by the game board, propped up on one elbow.

"We need to talk."

"About the squirrels?"

"Yes. I want to know more about that drug!"

He walked around and sat across the board from her, legs crossed Indian style, his fingers lightly folded before him as he leaned toward her.

"Why?"

"Why?" she asked with amazement. "Because I have an eight-year-old son, and there are animals copulating all over my property!"

"That's nature, Katrina."

"The hell it is! What—"

"What you really want to know is what effect the drug had on you, isn't it?"

It seemed that there was a taunt to his voice; and it had been exactly what she was worrying about, wondering about. She felt herself turn red; she longed to lash out and slap him. But he seemed to guess her intention, and before she could move, the little balls from the Hungry, Hungry Hippos game were suddenly streaking all across the tile, and she was on her back, with him straddled over her, carefully, warily holding her wrists to her side.

"Get off of me!"

"Un-unh. You're dangerous."

"I am not."

"You are."

"Well, I'm going to be a whole bunch more so if you—"

She broke off. She didn't want him looking at her so intently. She didn't want to feel the heat of his thighs around her, or the strength of his hands wound around her wrists, feeling the race of her pulse. She didn't want to stare up at his chest, gleaming in the candlelight, or into his eyes, strange as smoke, or see the rueful twist of his lips, a smile that managed to be both threatening and amused and richly sensual.

"You were an angel, Mrs. Denver," he told her. "You slept like a log."

"Then why—why"—she closed her eyes, then opened them again—"why was I—"

"Naked?"

"Yes, Captain Taylor," she drawled sarcastically. "That is the word."

He laughed and shrugged. "Honestly, I must have dozed off. I don't know exactly when you removed it." He was being sincere; she believed him. But then his voice changed. "Maybe you were—hot."

"You—"

"Behave, Mrs. Denver!" he warned, his fingers tightening around her wrists.

She pursed her lips together and managed to kick him in the back with her heel. Her position was so twisted that she couldn't have caused him much harm. She only seemed to amuse him.

Amuse him—and set him into motion, rolling, coming back into a position where his legs pinned hers, where his fingers twined with hers, where his torso, his face, came to just a breath above her own.

She knew that it was coming long before it did. It was a moment forever ingrained in her mind in which his smile slowly faded, and the lazy smoke filled his eyes as he drank in hers. She was barely aware that his fingers left hers; keenly aware that they caressed her cheek, held her chin. She felt his lips, even before they touched hers, knew that they would be firm, that they would savor and caress, would not accept denial, would be tender and persuasive, then burst to fire. He knew her lips, parted them, tasted the texture of her teeth, and delved all the warm secrets beyond. Her heartbeat merged with his in the sweet fever of their mouths, in the wonderful pressure of his body that was so achingly good against hers.

She was afraid to trust him; she couldn't help but do so. Her fingers slid into the hair at his nape, his caressed her cheek and wound to her shoulder, pulling her closer. He moved away from her slightly, his breath still warm against her, his eyes a question, gentle, tender and strong, on hers.

"You're beautiful," he told her huskily. "I think I—"

"No!" she cried suddenly, savagely. Because that was when her eyes left his—and fell on the photo on the mantel.

James. She was making a mockery of what they had shared. All the years she had lived on memories, and now, in two days, she was ready and willing and eager! to be with another man!

She was ready to fight him with fury, but she didn't have to. He had rolled away, was gone already, standing with his back to her, staring at the portrait.

"He's dead," he told her flatly. Then he spun around, hunched down on one knee, taking her hands and bringing her up. "And since you're so concerned about animals, Mrs. Denver, I should remind you that the human being is one. Flesh and blood and instinct and raw nerves, but more too. Much more. Memory and thought and feeling. More than any cat of the jungle, any snake, any predator, a human is an animal to be handled carefully. Don't tread on instinct, Mrs. Denver, and don't tread on emotion. It's a dangerous thing to do, because the most gentle of beasts can be provoked into rage."

"I didn't provoke you into anything! I—"

"You kissed me back. You almost, almost, came to life. But you don't want that, do you? You think that by being self-sacrificing you can make up for the fact that you're not dead. The lowest animal knows, Mrs. Denver, that that isn't God's way, or nature's."

"Let me go! I'm not an animal! I'm not a subject for you to study and analyze! Let me—"

"Run, Mrs. Denver? You can't run from life—or from

emotion. But if you're so determined, by all means go ahead. I won't stop you."

She did run. Literally. And she didn't stop until she was in her bedroom, with the door closed and locked.

CHAPTER SIX

Her heart would not stop racing; nor would her ragged breathing cease.

She stood at her door awhile, simply feeling. She realized suddenly—or perhaps not so suddenly—that running was not what she had wanted to do at all. She realized that she wanted him, wanted to respond to him, wanted to overcome the guilt and confusion and just touch, and be touched, and . . .

No! She left the door, scrambled blindly in the top drawer of her dresser, and found a flashlight. A shower would be nice. A cold shower, to remind her that this was not reality, that gentle pink clouds could only embrace one in dreams, that surely, real love happened only once in a lifetime.

The flashlight led her to the bathroom. She shed her jeans and T-shirt and climbed into the stall, glad of the cold, glad of the shocking punishment against her heated flesh. And she stayed there, scrubbing herself over and over again with the bar of soap.

At last she turned the water off. She could hear the wind then, louder than it had seemed during the day. She toweled herself dry with the same heated energy with which she had washed.

And it was then that she paused. She noticed that her skin smelled of the soap: clean, with just a touch of perfume. It made her feel very sleek and feminine, just like a woman who was awaiting a lover.

Lover. What a funny word. She'd never had a "lover," only a husband she had loved, a husband who was gone. She was alone now, and she needed to be held. She wanted to explore the man in the next room, who had fascinated her from the very first with his silver eyes, and filled her dreams. And she saw it all again: going to him, entering his room, his arms coming out to her.

He wanted her. Surely, he wanted her. He had kissed her, held her, and only her scream of denial and fury had broken them apart. It could happen; she could just go to him, embrace the darkness, touch him, and feel his touch.

A burst of agony and doubt swept through her then. But she was already moving. Her palms were drenched; she wiped them on the towel she had knotted around herself. The agony, the doubt, stayed with her. In the fantasy she could see herself walking, she could see his arms, but nothing more. She didn't know how to seduce, how to cajole, how to be sultry. It had been too long.

But still, she was moving. Her heart was pounding like a storm.

Her hand was on the doorknob, and then the door was open. The house was dark; the only light was from a flashlight that had been left standing on the coffee table.

She took a step, then another, and another, her bare feet touching the cool tiles.

Right before she reached his door, she panicked. What if he had locked it?

But his door wasn't locked. Her face tightened into a mask of pain as her fingers faltered upon it. *Open it!* she commanded herself.

At last she did; the door swung inward. More darkness greeted her, more and more. Her feet no longer wanted to move, but they did, step after slow, silent step. She could just make out the shape of the bed and the shape of his body beneath the sheets.

And then she was standing over him, and somehow, she knew that he was awake, that he was half sitting up, that he was watching her, and that he saw far more in the dark than she did.

A small sound escaped her; she wanted to run again as his

hand came out of the darkness and his fingers wound around her wrist.

"Good evening, Mrs. Denver."

He wasn't supposed to speak.

"I—I just wanted to say I'm sorry."

"The hell you did. You came to make love."

She wanted to die. Or fall to the floor and crawl away.

She could do neither; he was up and next to her and she felt the entire naked length of his body as he swept her into his arms, then down to the bed. In the darkness she could see the silver glow of his eyes and feel the tension that hardened the fine lines of his face into a taut mask.

"I'm not your husband, Mrs. Denver," he told her bluntly.

"Please—"

"Not this time, Mrs. Denver."

She felt his hand, tugging at the knot of her towel. The towel fell away; then she felt his fingers again on her cheek, moving between her breasts, stroking her stomach with velvet tenderness.

"I'm more than willing to play stud service for you, Mrs. Denver," he said so softly that it took seconds for her mesmerized mind to react, for her body to tense, for her hands to lash out to push him away. He didn't appear to notice; his leg was locked over hers, his manhood, hard and alive with a vibrant pulse, touched her thigh. His hands caught hers easily, drew them together, held them as the warm and arousing touch of his lips played over her forehead, against the lobe of her ear, the static pulse at the base of her throat.

"More than willing. But there will be some honesty in the situation."

Suddenly, he was gone from her. She heard the strike of a match, saw a flare in the night. She closed her eyes with absolute horror, aware that he had lit the candle by his bed and that the glow fell upon her.

She had entered the lion's den, and the lion had no intention of letting her loose.

His arm clamped around her waist; he held her there, forcing her to meet his eyes.

"I didn't want—light!" she managed to choke out, and he smiled, a little grimly.

"Ah! Honesty."

"All right! I came to—I came to you, but I changed my mind—"

"Too late."

"Jason! My son is—"

"Sound asleep, Katrina. I checked on him, Katrina. His door is closed—as is this one. You can't hide behind him now."

She lowered her head and moaned softly. Tears suddenly filled her eyes, but he ignored them, gently forcing her back down to the sheets. She closed her eyes, aware that if she opened them, she would see him studying her in the candle glow from head to toe.

His fingers were on her again, caressing her the way his eyes were caressing her, curving softly around her breasts, grazing her nipples to taut peaks, rubbing over her belly and then her thighs until she was longing for him to touch her further, again and again, deeper.

"Look at me, Katrina."

"Please . . ."

"Look at me!"

Her eyes opened at his ruthless command. He was still touching her, arousing her breast with just the stroke of his thumb, barely there, making her ache, burn inside, deep inside.

"Watch me. Watch me touch you."

"You have no mercy!" she choked out.

He smiled, hiking his left eyebrow slightly. "I've lots of mercy, Katrina. You just can't see that now. But—you will see me."

His head dipped to her breast. She felt his mouth on her nipple, his tongue sliding around it, a gentle suction that swept into her like molten mercury, making her body shudder and shake, her fingers grasp his hair, a soft cry escape her. Nor did he end it there. With gentle, sweeping force, he administered to her left breast as completely, slid the hard length of his body next to hers, captured her mouth with passion. She was aching; she was not ready for the kiss to break. It did, because his body was moving against hers again, his tongue washing over her belly, his teeth grazing her hip. He moved her and positioned her and she responded to his slightest touch, twisting, catching his hair, gasping, trembling ardently.

She felt his hand moving between her thighs. Then his fingers were teasing her, suddenly inside of her, rhythmic, deep, touching that core that was alive and hot with sweet fire. And his face was against her breasts again, and he was telling her how sweet she smelled, like the flowers after a rain, like the air at sea, like something totally edible and so delicious.

She thought that she would die if he did not ease the hunger that had grown in her. She had lost all fear, all sense of right or wrong, all reason; she wanted him so desperately.

But then he was suddenly gone; not really gone, but no longer touching her. He had risen high above her, his weight held by the corded muscles in his arms. She had writhed and twisted and arched to him, wantonly, shamelessly, and now he was staring at her again. Her lashes fluttered down quickly.

"Open your eyes!" he ordered her.

She did—belligerently, defiantly, ready to cry with fury, with loss, with confusion.

He smiled slowly and lazily, so very aware of what he had done to her, exactly how he had made her feel.

"I'm not your husband. Don't pretend that I am. Touch me. Know that I'm different. That I'm Michael Taylor."

"Oh!" she choked out miserably, and tried to twist away.

He wouldn't let her. He fell against her, capturing her face between his hands, kissing her long and fully again, and rekindling fires that still burned with a vengeance.

Then he looked at her again, caressing her cheeks with both hunger and tenderness.

"I am not your husband. But I am a man who finds you beautiful and exotic, and so sensually arresting that I would gladly be doomed to a thousand hells just to touch you. A man who could love you every bit as deeply and well, if you would just give him a chance."

The movement of his mouth against hers was slow and leisurely, open-mouthed kisses that touched and broke away, kisses that she tried to capture, that she returned.

"Touch me," he told her again, and she did, her fingers shimmering along his sides, along his back. *Know the difference!* he seemed to be commanding her, and she did. He was broad and tautly muscled, and her hands shook to adore the vital, powerful feel of him. He wasn't James; she loved being with him. *Him.* Loved the tapering feel of his torso, the tautness of his waist.

"Want me?" he asked her suddenly, hoarsely.

She nodded, not bothering to close her eyes.

"Take me."

And she did. Her fingers closed around him, stroking him, drawing him, the hot fluid core within her flaring ever brighter with his shudders, his groans of pleasure.

Then he was sheathed within her, a vital, fluid part of her, with strokes that promised, strokes that withheld, movement, rhythm, swift and powerful, growing. He was drawing her ever higher into a whirlwind of ecstasy, making it last and last, creating a raging sea of sensation, until she thought she would explode with it, until she did explode with it, in a moment so bright that it seemed that stars burst all around her in prisms of beautiful, blinding delight, delight matched only by the feel of him finding that same delight within her, flooding her with a sea of himself.

And even then, even then, she felt as if she were cradled within the beautiful, warm depths of a tropic sea, held, cherished, soothed. She was floating down on clouds—not pink ones, but clouds that were as sheer as silk, tender, gentle clouds, easing the beat of her heart, the gasp of her breath.

He touched her hair, smoothed it from her face. Then he smiled at her, tenderly and openly.

And then, only then, did he snuff out the candle. And then, only then, did it seem he had no words.

But neither did she. She was content to lie beside him, savoring the feel of his body, basking in the knowledge of his masculinity. She loved the strength of his arm, so comfortable around her.

But in time, she stirred.

"I've got to get back to my own room. Jason—"

He held her tight and kissed her forehead. "Trust me. I awake at exactly six A.M. like clockwork. Stay beside me."

"But—"

His mouth found hers. He spoke between kisses. "Trust me. Let me love you again."

Trust me. She clung to the words, because she couldn't deny him. She was attuned to him, alive to his touch, and already she was more than eager to be loved again.

Apparently, Mike Taylor did have a body alarm clock; he awoke her at exactly six. She desisted at first, lazily trying to curl back into his arms, then glanced at her wristwatch. Two minutes past six on the nose.

She kissed him quickly, was pulled back into his warm, warm embrace, and then released. Grabbing her towel, she retreated to her own room and promptly, very contentedly, returned to a deep sleep.

She awoke again because it was light, beautifully, brilliantly light. The storm was past, and Mike had apparently reopened the shutters.

She smiled, stretched lethargically, then froze again, wondering how she was going to face him this morning, then wondering how she was going to bear it when he went away.

Don't think about it yet! she pleaded with herself. *Just let it be; appreciate all that he has done for you, for your belief in yourself.*

She didn't even want to ponder that last thought, so she jumped out of bed, took a quick, cold shower, and dressed in shorts and a halter top. With the sun streaming so brilliantly, it was sure to be scorching hot.

She really didn't let herself think as she hurriedly brushed her well-tousled hair, then rushed out of her room. She had to face him in daylight—and do it quickly, before she could retreat behind a new wall of rational thinking.

She forced herself to think of what an absolutely beautiful day it was as she walked down the hall; it was so very, very bright after all the darkness. Was everything exceptionally beautiful and perfect today, or was it just her, seeing it all with new eyes, eyes that had been reopened by a man named Michael Taylor?

Mike was in the kitchen with Jason, showing him how to make toast on a griddle. His eyes rose instantly from his task and met hers across the room. Then he gave her a smile that was deep, a smile that denied nothing, that made her feel uniquely wonderful and glad to be alive.

She walked into the kitchen. "Want some eggs to go with that toast?" she asked cheerfully.

"Mornin', Mom!" Jason said.

Mike lifted his brows. "Don't you think the eggs might be bad by now?"

"Nonsense!" she replied briskly, and she wondered if her eyes were sparkling like his, reflecting the sweet, intimate secret they shared. "Some of us think to put the beer in the freezer. Then some of us move the eggs in as well!"

Jason laughed with delight. Katrina got out the eggs and decided that the American cheese would be okay, too, and that she could make omelettes.

Mike handed her a cup of coffee over the counter, then leaned against it, still smiling lazily, leisurely.

"Coffee every morning," she commented. "Maybe you're not so bad to have around."

"Coffee," he replied, "is easy. I perk right along with it when I—sleep as well as I did last night."

Her fingers trembled slightly, just from a graze with his. She felt a little dizzy, just from breathing the air around him. He touched the air with his scent, with his presence.

"Eggs," she murmured aloud, and promptly dropped the first one she picked up.

"Mom!" Jason laughed, hurrying for a paper towel. "She's really not a klutz!" he informed Mike so solemnly that Katrina had to smile as she bent to help her son clean the floor. *Oh, Jason, I like him too. You're too young to understand how much!*

"Maybe I should handle the eggs—" Mike was starting to say, but he never finished the sentence, because there was a loud rapping against the kitchen wall, a voice that called out, and the sudden appearance of an old, old man.

" 'Trina, Jason, you in there?"

"Harry!"

Katrina was quickly on her feet, ready to greet him. Harry Anderson was a good friend to her and Jason. He was small and bony with a thin, gaunt face, but he had eyes of so bright a blue that they defied age. According to him, he had been born somewhere between 1895 and the turn of the century. He was wrinkled like an old peach, but he was as spry as a pup. Due to good living, he'd told her once: a shot of good whiskey before bed every night, a pipeful of Cherry tobacco after dinner, and women—except that they didn't seem to be making them his age anymore!

"Harry? How did you get here?"

"I got worried about you in the storm, so I motored on out. Who and what in tarnation are you there, then, sonny?"

Katrina wanted to laugh; Mike seemed so startled at being referred to as "sonny." But he took it all in stride, stepping forward to offer Harry his hand.

"Captain Michael Taylor, sir, U.S.N."

Harry studied Michael carefully, then took the hand offered to him. He gazed at Katrina again. "This boy's got a grip like a damned bull mastiff. Must be all right. Friend of yours?"

"Ah—yes, a marooned friend," she lied. Her eyes met Jason's rather than Mike's. Her son's gaze answered her own, and she realized that she had already told her first lie in Mike's defense.

"That your boat on the shore, son?"

Mike's eyes widened with excitement. "Washed up—on the shore? It's not broken to bits?"

Harry shook his head. "It's dug itself straight into the beach. Sitting at a slant, though. And there's a hole in her hull; I'm not too sure she'll ever be seaworthy again."

Mike shook his head. "That doesn't really matter—there's just some things I might be able to get off of her." He turned to Katrina. "I'm going down to see what I can get. If you see a bunch of men in uniform next, don't get panicky." He gazed at Harry and grimaced. "The Navy, you know. They'll be looking for me."

He waved quickly and left them. Harry watched him go, then turned to Katrina. "I'm going to motor on back to the main island, young lady, and give your folks a call. Your phone's been out, and your ma and pa have been frantic."

"Oh, Harry, bless you!" Katrina said gratefully.

"Can I ride over with Harry?" Jason asked.

"No," Katrina said instantly. The islands, she knew, would be a mess. There would be downed power lines everywhere, and flooded roads.

"Let him come with me," Harry urged her. "If his grandma hears his voice, she'll be real relieved. I'll go straight to the MacKenzie docks, and straight back. I'll watch him with me life, that I will!"

With both of them looking at her with huge, pleading eyes, Katrina consented. Harry would drop dead a thousand times over before he let anything happen to Jason. And Jason had more common sense than most grown-ups. He would be careful.

"Oh . . . all right," she agreed.

Then they, too, were gone. She sighed and started picking up the uneaten toast. She sipped her coffee, then jumped off her stool. Jason and Harry would be gone for a couple of hours. She was alone, with no responsibilities. If she wanted, she could actually run down to the beach and help Michael.

She didn't stop to decide whether or not he would want the help, she just ran. Or rather, she stumbled, picking her way through all the fallen debris.

A little breathlessly, she arrived on the beach. Just as Harry had said, the *Maggie Mae* was there, so deeply rooted into the sand that she might have been built there.

"Michael!" she called out, standing on the sand, her hand shielding her eyes from the sun.

He appeared on the deck, balancing carefully, since it was, indeed, on an angle.

"She's perfect!" he called down to Katrina excitedly. "Perfect! A few smashed cups, that's it!"

"Can I help?"

"No, but come aboard! Every man likes to work with a beautiful woman around!"

Katrina stepped forward. He reached down to help her, catching her arms, pulling her straight over the rim with little effort.

"You're just flattering me!" she protested.

He held her against him so that the hair on his chest tickled her nose. "I meant it, Katrina!" he whispered huskily. Then he broke from her, frowning. "Where's Jason?"

She smiled. "Gone to Islamorada with Harry. It will be at least a two-hour trip." She wrinkled her nose slightly. "Jason has to talk to my mother. That could take forever."

"Troubled waters there?"

"Oh, no! I love Mathilda to death. But if you think I'm something to tangle with, you should meet Matty on a tangent!"

Mike laughed, then hugged her again. "Two hours," he said thickly. "Give me fifteen minutes here, and then we'll have a hundred and five of them anywhere you want."

With a wicked smile he turned and ducked back into the cabin. Katrina stared up at the sun for a minute, then followed him in. He wasn't in the galley; she heard him rummaging around in his sleeping quarters.

She started to pick up the broken cups.

"Katrina."

Startled, Katrina turned around. He had come out of the cabin and was leaning against the door, staring at her with a look so tense that it brought chills to her spine.

"Michael?"

"I have to tell you something."

"What?" she demanded, suddenly very wary.

He swallowed miserably and came toward her. Before he spoke, she knew that she wanted to run—again—from a new pain she didn't understand.

"Katrina, I have to tell you about the boat. The drug. You see, you pulled at my mask. I was hit with it too. The dreams that you were having—that is, you and I—"

She inhaled in a desperate, pained gasp, and exhaled in a scream. "Oh, my God! It was real! You used me! You—"

"No, damn you! It wasn't like that—"

She wrenched away from him and clutched the nearest thing and threw it at him; it was a piece of a shattered mug. He was too startled and confused to duck; it caught him right across the forehead, leaving a thin strip of blood.

"I'll kill you!" she raged. "You told me to trust you! You liar! You hoax! You bastard!"

"Katrina, it wasn't—"

"You used me! And then you lied! Oh, my Lord, you took the worst advantage of me possible! You and your pink clouds! Oh! I swear I'll see you in jail for the rest of your life! How could you? And the things that you said last night! You liar! What were you trying to do? Cover your tracks? Get me into bed willingly just in case there were any—were any . . ."

"Were any what?" he demanded furiously, his lips pressed so tightly together then that they were white.

"Repercussions!" she shouted. "Oh! I hate you! I—"

Her fingers closed around another piece of broken mug. She threw it, and then another, and another. She could barely see; she was blinded with rage and by her tears.

But he was expecting her fury now; he ducked all her missiles easily, then started coming for her.

"No!" she yelled, aware at last that he was bleeding at the forehead and bore a look that threatened definite violence. She turned and stumbled out of the cabin. She crawled to the bow gunwale and jumped down to the sand. It was farther than she had expected, and she fell face first into it. Sputtering, she tried to get to her knees.

His weight sent her sprawling downward again. He rolled her over, straddled her, and pinned her down, every bit as furious as she had been.

"Stop it, Katrina!"

Tears stung her eyes; her heart pounded unbearably, she desperately wanted to get away from him.

"Don't! You can quit the act now! You—"

"I didn't do a damn thing! You came to me!"

"It was your stinking drug!"

"Yes, damn it, and thanks to you, I'd gotten a bit myself."

"So that's what it is! You are insane! What, is this drug something to cheer up manic depressives, or is it a war weapon? Oh, my God, the Russians will just love you when they find themselves copulating like animals all over the place."

"They'd love me a whole lot less if they were walking around maimed and bleeding and dying of radiation sickness! And the damned thing isn't perfected yet! It works on the mind by acting on dreams and ideals that are already there! Damn you, Katrina! If you hadn't been indulging in fantasies you were afraid to live, it might not—"

"You bastard!"

"You knew it! It doesn't erase memory! You knew damned well that you'd been with me!"

"No!" She shook her head furiously in denial. "Oh, and I hate you more for last night. It was a lie! It was such a damn lie. All done to cover—"

"Cover what?"

"I told you."

"Told me what?"

"In case I'd gotten pregnant the other time," she spat out.

"Pregnant! You do have the mind of a pure shrew! Last night happened because you wanted me and I wanted you," Mike insisted angrily.

"How could I want you when I totally loathe you?" Katrina cried, tears welling in her eyes.

"You are a coward, and the worst liar I've ever known, because you're even willing to lie to yourself!"

"The only liar around here is you! You told me to trust you, and you're nothing but a sham—just like last night, just like everything that goes on between us."

Suddenly he grabbed her and kissed her hungrily; then he let her go, leaving her trembling, breathless. "Now do you want to tell me that last night was a sham?"

His fingers were in her hair; she had no chance to reply, because as soon as her mouth opened, his covered it again. There was anger in his kiss, but something more, something so yearning and fierce that it couldn't be denied.

Then his lips were gone from hers, and he was looking at her passionately.

"I won't let you go! I won't let you retreat again! Listen to me! He is dead! Your husband is dead! But it's him you betray if you refuse to love again. You discredit everything that was ever good and beautiful between you. I'm sorry for the foul-up. I'm sorry for the pink cloud. But I'm not sorry I touched you, and I swear that I will not stop!" He paused, his breath ragged. "Dammit, I care! And I need you!"

That was it; those last frustrated words, the desperation in them, the emotion, electric and potent, touching her. And it was more. It was the pure explosion of passion, nurtured to volcanic levels by the tension between them. His lips found hers again, his hands were touching her.

And there was nothing left to deny. She had no reason, no sense, not even pride. She was suddenly touching him, too, winding her arms around his neck, pressing against him, loving him, as eager to shed her clothing beneath the sun as he was to remove it. She was desperate to be a part of him.

They soared to a brilliant place above the anger, above the pain. They were barely aware that the surf played over their feet, that the sand covered their bodies, that gulls and pelicans flew above them. The flame that rose between them flared, burned, crested, leaving them tangled together in the sand, just breathing, panting, stunned—and suddenly quite silent.

At last, Mike rolled away from her. He stood, and pulled his trousers back on. He walked out to the surf, letting it soak his legs, staring out to sea.

His back was to her. "Katrina . . . I . . ."

"Ahoy, there!" a voice called out.

Mike ducked, then raced back to Katrina, bringing her the scattered pieces of her clothing. She pushed him away in a flurry of humiliation and rolled ridiculously into the surf to dress.

"Ahoy, there—Michael?"

"Admiral, I'm here," he said. He walked around the bow slowly, stalling for time.

Then another name came from his lips, stated with something far less than pleasure.

"Albert, what in the hell are you doing here?"

CHAPTER SEVEN

Katrina was dripping wet when she emerged from the surf, and feeling absolutely ridiculous.

But it could have been much worse, she realized. The men in uniform could have appeared just five minutes earlier.

There were three of them, all in white, standing on the other side of the beached bow of the *Maggie Mae.* One was an older man, stiff and straight with snow-white hair beneath his cap, worn and creased features, and pleasant green eyes.

He had the most stripes and insignias on his shirt sleeves, but they wouldn't have been needed to tell even the most casual observer that he was the one with rank, the man in charge.

Not that the second man looked in the least humble.

He was somewhere between thirty and forty, tall, lean, and striking with blond hair and very blue eyes, a straight nose, and a sandy mustache. There was something about him that bothered Katrina; he seemed too confident, to the point of utter arrogance.

Suddenly she looked at Mike, and the pain of his betrayal streaked through her again. She didn't blame him for what had just happened, but she wasn't sure she could forgive him for what had happened on the boat. She still might very well hate him. She just didn't know; she felt torn in a million pieces, adrift, as battered as the palms that lay about the island.

"Mrs. Denver, Admiral Larson, Captain Stradford, Lieutenant Oberon," Mike was saying. And before she stepped forward to accept the admiral's hand with her sandy and dripping one, she stared at Mike. His eyes were pure, hard, proud steel. And she knew right then that if she decried him, he would stand still and listen, and admit to every truth. He wouldn't lie or hedge or make any denial.

She accepted the admiral's hand, the captain's, then the lieutenant's. It might have been a cocktail party. She might have been neatly decked out in silk rather than in sopping wet cotton shorts.

"Mrs. Denver!" The admiral had her hand again. "There is nothing that can undo the terrible negligence that has occurred; I can only offer you our most sincere apologies and seek to rectify the damage done. We will, I promise you, get to the bottom of this unforgiveable error!"

Mike was standing back slightly, arms crossed over his bare chest. "Mrs. Denver is considering a legal suit, sir."

Captain Stradford emitted something like a snort. "I warned you, sir! This was bound to—"

"Stradford!" The admiral lifted a hand into the air. "We do not air our dirty laundry in public!"

Did she still intend to sue? Mike obviously thought that she did. She didn't know; she didn't know what would be right or wrong, and most awful of all, she didn't even know what she felt, except for the pain and rage still simmering within her. She wanted to hurt him, just as she felt hurt—but something warned her to take care, because she didn't want him really injured in terms of his career. What she felt was private, not to be aired in public, just as the admiral had said.

Still, she was too angry to let Mike off the hook completely.

"Admiral," she said smoothly, "I'm reserving judgement until I have a better understanding of the situation. When you've offered me further information, I'll be in a better position to decide on my personal beliefs."

"Quite right, Mrs. Denver," the admiral said. "And, of course, I intend to speak with you. Will you be so good as to join me for lunch aboard ship?"

He indicated a large ship out on the horizon, not too far from where the *Maggie Mae* had once been.

Katrina hesitated, then murmured, "If you can excuse me for about thirty minutes . . ."

Her words drew attention to her drenched state. Mike stepped into the conversation smoothly.

"We were trying to salvage some things from the *Maggie Mae,*" he said flatly.

"Of course, of course!" the admiral said, and then he was staring at Mike's soaked, rolled-up trousers, bare chest, and disarrayed sandy hair.

"You're a bit of a mess yourself, Taylor," the admiral said.

"Yes, sir."

"Stradford—you can escort the lady to her home and back to the beach. We'll have transport waiting. Lunch at thirteen hundred."

"I can make my own way back to my house."

"Nonsense, Mrs. Denver! After all we've done, the least we can offer is escort!"

He had already turned, walking briskly for a dinghy onshore with a sailor standing by. Albert Stradford grinned at Mike as if he had won some victory.

"Shall we, Mrs. Denver?" he asked, inclining his head slightly.

Katrina determined to smile with all her charm at Stradford, just to put Mike in his place.

But then, she quickly became sorry that she had tried out her charm on Stradford. He seemed to think that it made them conspirators.

He strode ahead of her, taking his role as escort to heart, moving palm fronds, breaking off sea-grape branches to make her walk entirely smooth.

"Mrs. Denver"—he was breathing a little heavily in his efforts to slash through the foliage like a uniformed Tarzan—"I'd like to add my personal apologies for all that you've been through."

"Thank you, Captain," she said crisply, "but actually, I haven't been through anything that terrible."

He made a sound of disgust. "You must have been frightened, worried. And with a son . . ."

Yes, she had been terrified, worried sick. But she wasn't about to let Stradford know that.

"As I said, Captain, things haven't been so bad."

"You should sue him!" Stradford advised her.

"It's the Navy I'd be suing, Captain."

He shrugged, offering her a smile that was meant to entice and seduce along with his striking blond looks. "The Navy, yes, and of course, I'd hate to see that. But really, we can't run around, irresponsibly testing out drugs!" He shook his head. "Taylor is a little bit crazy. I'm still amazed that they listen to him."

"The admiral must believe in him," Katrina said politely.

Stradford stopped, right in the middle of the trail. "You could change things, Mrs. Denver. If you made a stink, they'd stop. They'd can this whole ridiculous project."

"Maybe it's not such a bad project," she murmured.

He started off through the foliage again, not pleased.

In another few moments they were back to the house. She invited him in, a little awkwardly. He thanked her, gave her another of his charming smiles, and made himself comfortable on her couch.

Katrina showered quickly. She washed her hair and blew it dry. She was suddenly quite determined to look her best, and as sophisticated as possible. She applied some makeup, then tore into her closet until she decided on a pale-blue knit suit and matching pumps—ones with nice high heels to make her feel just a little bit taller, a little more level with the score of men who had descended on her island.

She wound her wild, long hair up into a knot on the top of her head and convinced herself she had achieved a little height and a little dignity and age. She wanted the admiral to know that he was dealing with an adult, and she wanted Mike to believe that she would carry out any threat she might issue.

Tears suddenly stung her eyes. "I hate you, Mike Taylor!" she whispered. "I really, really hate you!"

But there was another voice inside of her, denying the words.

I just don't want you to go away! I just want to believe in you, I want to be able to—to what? she wondered.

The answer was one she couldn't accept: *love again.*

She turned away from her mirror and hurried out to meet Stradford.

He stood as soon as he saw her, and smiled appreciatively.

"Wish I'd been marooned with you throughout Kathleen," he told her wistfully.

"Thank you, Captain, I'll take that as a compliment."

"It was definitely meant as one. By the way, my name is Al."

She nodded her head slightly. "Al."

"Well, I guess we'd better get going." He opened the door for her.

On the way to the beach he complimented her on her house, the island, and her life-style. Katrina wondered what he knew about her life-style, then remembered with a spurt of irritation that the Navy seemed to know quite a bit about her.

On paper, yes! Only one of them really knew her, knew her so well that even the thought of it was enough to send her head reeling, her body quivering, her temper soaring.

It was when they actually reached the beach—just inches away from the *Maggie Mae*—that Katrina suddenly balked. "Captain Stradford—I can't leave here. My son and a friend went over to Islamorada. I've got to wait for them to get back."

Stradford frowned. "They're off the island?"

"Yes."

"Taylor let them get off the island?"

"Captain!" Katrina breathed with exasperation. "As far as I know, this is still a free country!"

"Yes, yes!" Stradford assured her, smiling. "It's just that discretion is important at the moment."

Katrina arched a brow. "I thought you were against the

experiment anyway, Captain. Why should you care what happens?"

"I am against the experiment, but, then, there is protocol. And if your little boy is spreading tales everywhere—"

"The boy isn't running around spreading tales!" a deep voice said irritably. Katrina almost jumped, she was so startled. She looked up against the bright sunlight of day. Mike Taylor was standing on the deck of the yacht, staring downward, his eyes hard as steel, his hands clenched tightly around the railing. He'd apparently showered and changed, and once again, in a neat white uniform with blue trim and epaulets, he appeared extremely formidable. His face looked tanned and hard and grim; he seemed to be staring at them both with distaste.

The blood suddenly seemed to run cold throughout her, and she couldn't help returning to her earlier thoughts. Conflicting thoughts.

You opened the world to me again. . . .

You used me!

Abruptly, he moved, muscled arms creating leverage as he leapt over the bow to land smoothly in the sand in front of Katrina. "I'll wait here for Jason and Harry," he told her. "Go ahead"—his voice carried a hard note of sarcasm—"I'm sure you'd like to get started with the admiral."

"Yes, I suppose I would," she said coolly.

He inclined his head just slightly toward the other man. "Al—the lady awaits."

They really seem to hate one another, Katrina thought, and she was torn enough to want to use her knowledge to the fullest limit.

She smiled sweetly at the handsome blond captain with the sandy mustache. "Yes, Captain, as long as Taylor here is willing to wait for my son, I would just love to get started."

She turned, managing to discreetly catch her heel in the sand and issue a soft little cry. Al Stradford was right there, ready to grab her arm and support her.

Katrina resisted the temptation to turn around and see Mike's reaction.

Al Stradford carefully helped her into the motor launch. As they whirred out to meet the admiral, he shouted to her conversationally above the roar of the boat and the whip of the wind, pointing to the Navy vessel.

"She's a specially outfitted cutter!" he told her, grinning. "The admiral's pride and joy. You'll see why!"

The admiral was waiting for her on deck, very graciously. She might have been a close friend, so cordial was his manner as he showed her around, introducing her now and then to a sailor or an officer. There were, she learned, more than twenty crew members aboard. They were all with a special joint unit of the Armed Forces devoted for the time being to research. Some of them were Marines, and some of them were Navy.

Katrina mentioned that she found that unusual. The admiral laughed. "Not at all, young lady. We're really all in this together, whatever rivalry there might be! Air Defense is an Army group, but you'll find them at Air Force bases most of the time!"

The cutter was the U.S.S. *Elizabeth;* she had been designed for meetings among the brass in 1940, refitted in 1983 to modern standards.

"Ah, but she's still a glorious vessel!" the admiral told Katrina, openly admiring the ship's sleek lines. "The galley is a piece of modern art, the dining room is as classic as the ages—but come, you'll see."

Al Stradford left them when they entered an elegant cabin at the bow, just below the helm. There were two places set at the table: one for her, one for the admiral.

"A drink, Mrs. Denver? Sherry? Wine?"

"A glass of Chablis, if I may, Admiral," she murmured.

He brought her a glass of wine; then, smiling, led her to a chair at the head of the table. He was, she realized, quite purposely trying to charm her; but he was doing it very openly, and they both knew it. And he had something going for him; he reminded her of her father. She also liked his eyes, with their wisdom and their deep look of humanity.

They were served by a polite and very correct sailor introduced to Katrina as Chief Petty Officer Gordon. He brought salads and a rich savory stew, then very discreetly disappeared.

Halfway into the dinner the admiral began his appeal.

"Mrs. Denver, I repeat my most profound apologies. And I'll swear again by your right to bring suit against the Navy. But you told me that you wanted to reserve opinion. I'm asking you now to do just that."

"Admiral, someone called me and told me it was all off. It wasn't anyone I knew, because I was asked not to tell anyone anything and I didn't. Something is going on here, and it certainly wasn't my fault, and I truly don't appreciate what happened!"

"Mrs. Denver, we know that. And we will discover what happened. Would it help you to know that we have full presidential approval for this experimentation? That Congress voted approval for the funding?"

"I—" What was this? An appeal to her patriotism? Yes, of course it was, she thought wearily.

"Science is slow moving, Mrs. Denver. As I said, this has been under way for years. Tested again and again in a laboratory. On mice, on chimps."

"Admiral, that's my point! My son and I are neither."

"But you see, I've been studying the results of 44DFS since its inception. It's true, Mrs. Denver. There are absolutely no lingering after-effects. It's as clean as a whistle. And . . . actually, we were ready to test on human beings. We were attempting to move as slowly and cautiously as possible."

Katrina played with her stew. "And you did wind up with humans," she murmured. *Oh, yes! Mike Taylor knows exactly what his drug can do!* she thought bitterly.

"Yes, we did," the admiral said, and she should have been prepared for what was coming. "You do have every right to be concerned, Mrs. Denver. A foreign substance—on you and your child."

"Yes."

"You wouldn't want to take anyone's word on lasting repercussions, would you?"

"It is hard to do, yes, Admiral."

"I can imagine. You see, we know all the effects on our lab animals, Mrs. Denver, because we watch them. We guarantee ourselves that no harm has come to their health."

"Commendable, Admiral."

"So, Mrs. Denver, I would assume then that—in deeply caring for the welfare of your son, and yourself, since you're alone to raise him—that you would be most anxious for us to take even greater care with human beings."

"I don't—"

"Mrs. Denver, I'd like you to agree to stay aboard the *Elizabeth.* Just for three days."

"No!" Katrina cried out in denial. She'd already been a guinea pig! What more did they want? She didn't want needles and pins and things stuck into her and Jason!

"Mrs. Denver, don't you want to be sure? Absolutely sure?"

"Why should I?" She demanded belligerently. "You've already assured me—"

"You've already been exposed to the substance. All we want to do is monitor your condition—"

"I don't have a condition!"

"Please, please! Mrs. Denver! Be reasonable! You have been exposed. All we want to do now is assure you and ourselves that we are right—that you are fine, that your son is fine."

"Oh, God!" She groaned. "This isn't fair!"

"Neither is warfare, Mrs. Denver," the admiral said tiredly. "And I've seen a lot of it! World War II, the Korean War, and Vietnam. I've seen the results of guns, atom bombs, napalm . . . I've seen it all, I've watched all kinds of things, conventional and modern. I'm not really telling you anything you don't know already, Mrs. Denver! 44DFS is the first humane weapon I've ever seen—a defensive weapon, Mrs. Denver. Can you think about that for a moment, please? And think about the repercussions if you don't give us a chance. It will be years and years before it's ever ready for any real military use, but doesn't the dream, just the idea itself, beat the hell out of total nuclear warfare?"

He had her; she was trapped. She opened up her mouth to speak; she couldn't.

He leaned across the table to her. "Mrs. Denver, am I asking so much? Three days of your time. All right, I want more than that, really. Three days of your time, and a little piece of your island to set up a small lab to study the water, the air, and the animals. A prefab structure. It will be gone in a month, I swear. And one more thing—your silence and cooperation for that month."

"Wait a minute!" Katrina protested.

"Mrs. Denver, is that so very much?"

"No. Yes! I don't know!" She hesitated, aware that her real disagreement was with Mike Taylor—the man, not the scientist. It was strictly, entirely personal. She did agree with the dream, didn't she, as fantastic as it all sounded?

The admiral kept talking and she kept stumbling for answers, and then suddenly, before she knew it, she had agreed to everything.

She didn't know exactly what happened next, because it all happened in an incredible whir. Someone was suddenly in the dining room with all kinds of papers. One young officer was a notary; he was there to witness her signature. Another was there to fully explain any of the legal terminology.

Amid it all, Katrina caught the admiral's eyes reproachfully. "I think I need a lawyer!" she told him bitterly.

"I can call one."

But it was really very simple. She read every line of the documents, discovered that there was no fine print, that she was agreeing to nothing more than had been said. There was even a clause that mentioned her full legal right to sue the Navy for previous negligence.

"Mrs. Denver, believe me, I'm not trying to trick you into anything. As God is my witness, Mrs. Denver, I'm still trying to get to the bottom of what happened in the first place!"

She started to place her wavering signature on the paper, but then she paused.

"Admiral, this isn't going to be so simple. There is my son to consider. I will not disrupt his life. Three days, yes, but I can't keep him out of school for a month."

"Mrs. Denver, we don't intend to deny that the Navy is working on your island, studying island life forms. After this week he'll be perfectly free to go back to school."

"Admiral, there's still going to be trouble. My in-laws live right across the water in Islamorada. They're going to be concerned; in fact, they'll probably be here soon. I work with my brother-in-law; do fishing charters, snorkeling parties, and teach scuba classes out on the reefs. And my parents live in Key West."

Nevertheless, Katrina found herself setting her signature to the paper. She had the strangest feeling that if she didn't, things would be taken out of her control anyway.

Mike frowned as he saw the dinghy approaching the shore. There were three people in it, not two: Jason, Harry, and a third man.

For a moment then, his heart began to beat quickly. He might have been seeing a ghost. The third man in the boat bore a striking resemblance to the picture on Katrina Denver's mantel, the picture of her husband.

"There's Mike!" Jason's excited voice came to him as the trio pulled the aging motor boat to the sand. Then he, Harry, and the other man were hurrying to him.

"Mike!" Jason cried. "This is my Uncle Frank. I told him we were okay, but he wanted to see Mom anyway."

Mike automatically stretched out a hand to the tall, thin man in jeans and T-shirt. A slight frown was bunching his dark brows, but there was a pleasant smile on his lips as he accepted Mike's hand and surveyed him openly.

"Frank Denver," he said, "Captain . . . ?"

"Taylor. Michael Taylor." Mike said, glad that Katrina's brother-in-law seemed to like what he saw. "I take it that you're . . ."

Frank laughed easily. "Yes, Trina's brother-in-law. I assume you saw the picture of James. There's just a strong family resemblance, huh, Jase?" He ruffled his nephew's hair affectionately, then looked back at Mike. "Jason said you were here through the storm, and I'd like to say that I'm grateful for your care of my sister-in-law and Jason."

Mike grimaced with pain. "They would have been better off without me," he said truthfully.

Frank shook his head. "The way it came up, so suddenly, it was just good to hear that they weren't alone. We usually evacuate even the main islands, Captain. Kat's house is as solid as a rock, but even so . . ." He shrugged, then frowned again. "Captain, what is going on here?"

"Mike," he replied automatically. "The Navy thought it had rented use of your sister-in-law's island, Mr. Denver—"

"Frank, please," the other man interrupted.

"We're, uh, studying wildlife," Mike said lamely.

"Mike, where's Mom?" Jason tugged at his hand.

Mike smiled down at him. "She's with the admiral."

"An admiral!" Jason's eyes lit up appreciatively. "A real one?"

Mike had to laugh. "Oh, yeah! I promise that Larson is real, very real! Want to come meet him?"

"Oh, boy!"

The admiral was going to get to handle this one, too, Mike decided grimly.

"Frank, want to come?"

"Definitely," the young man said.

Something touched Mike, something deep, that hurt. So this is what James Denver would have been like: tall, lean, browned by the sun, with dark eyes that were bright and keenly aware of the world, interested in everything, with a high capacity for laughter. Frank Denver couldn't have been more than twenty-five, but he had a sense of maturity about him.

I've just met him—and I like him, Mike realized. *I would have liked his brother.*

The man whose widow had stumbled into 44DFS. The

woman with whom he had become so passionately involved, who had come to him, and touched what he had thought was a heart of ice, long buried.

The woman who now wanted his scalp.

"Well, shall we go then? Harry, do you mind taking your boat over? They apparently decided not to send one back for us."

Harry saluted very properly. "Aye, Captain, at your service!"

"Yeah, let's go. I'm really anxious to see Katrina," Frank said.

So am I, Mike thought. *So am I!* His fingers curled into tight fists at his side. He knew he wouldn't see her. He didn't want to influence her decision in any way.

She had to do what she felt was right. If he saw her, he was going to want to touch her. If he touched her, she was going to believe that he was trying to sway her, when he simply—cared; when he just wanted to hold her, give her strength.

But she didn't want his strength. She wanted his neck!

CHAPTER EIGHT

Katrina had never seen things happen so quickly in her life. One minute she was in the gracious environment of the richly carved and paneled dining room with its Old World flair; the very next she found herself in a roomy but sterile cubicle.

Just as the papers had been ready for her, so had the room. There was a typical hospital-style bed, soothing music, a bedside stand, and even some kind of a VCR system—all incredibly neat and clean. Just like the white gown she'd been given to wear.

She'd been brought in by a nurse, a young lieutenant who was certainly one of the most beautiful women Katrina had ever met. She was sophisticated looking, with a perfectly made up face and a short cap of gleaming brown hair. Katrina had been given her rank and last name, but the nurse had cheerfully told her, "I do get so sick of titles! Please call me Amy!"

Amy had taken her blood pressure and her pulse, checked her temperature, and pricked her finger for a sample of blood. Then she had left her, promising that she was only a ring of the bedside buzzer away.

There was a cabin connected to hers, and Katrina had explored it with no hesitancy. It was, she knew, for Jason. She was a little stunned and resentful at the speed of things, and felt no qualms whatsoever about completely checking the room inside-out herself.

It was while she was in that room that a new man made an appearance in her life.

"Mrs. Denver?"

She walked through the connecting door to her own cabin and instantly decided that she liked the man who had addressed her. He was probably about five nine, slim and wiry, graying slightly, and good-natured looking, with a pair of gold-rimmed glasses that slid down his nose as he looked at her.

"Hi." He offered his hand. "Stan Thorpe, Mrs. Denver. I've come to talk to you about the phone call."

She told him about the call; he made notes. He muttered that the two officers sent to the island to make sure that it was clear should have found her anyway, shook his head, then smiled. "We will find out what happened, Mrs. Denver!" he promised her, and she felt like laughing because it was becoming such a standard promise.

"Can I get you anything? Coffee, tea, soda?"

She shrugged, not really wanting anything. Yet it seemed that he wanted an excuse to stay, so she asked for hot tea.

"Will do," he replied, pleased.

He returned with the tea quickly, and settled in the recliner across from the hospital bed.

"How did you fare through the storm, Mrs. Denver? We would have reached you much sooner without her blowing in, you know."

He was so pleasant, but she sensed that his conversation wasn't idle. And to her horror she blushed.

"We were fine through the storm. My house was built very sturdily, with lots of pilings. There was no flooding. And living here, I always have Sterno, canned stuff, candles, and the like." She hesitated a second, then asked bluntly, "Are you for the project?"

"I am."

"And—are you a friend of Captain Taylor's?"

He laughed. "Yeah, well, Mike and I go back a long way."

"Then what do you think of Captain Stradford? He doesn't seem to think too much of—of 44DFS—isn't that it?"

"Umm. 44DFS," Stan murmured. He shrugged again,

hunching forward a bit in his chair. "Al's a conventional kind of guy. He believes in old and tried and true methods—and he doesn't often feel kindly toward the enemy."

"Oh," Katrina murmured. "And that's why he's so against Mike Taylor?"

"No" was his unexpected answer. "Al and Mike just have bad chemistry." He grinned, studying her features. "We've all been career military. Al, Stan, and me. We've been around a lot together. I think if the chips were really down, the two of them would pull together. In fact, Mike pulled Al out of a burning ship once, back in Nam. Maybe it's hard to like the guy who saved you, I don't know. They're both good doctors, good men. They just have this thing about each other, you know."

"Two forty-year-olds acting like kids?"

Stan chuckled sheepishly. "Kind of."

"What is it that you want to know from me, Stan?" Katrina asked him softly.

He had the grace to blush. "I guess I want to know what you're feeling about the whole thing."

"Did Captain Taylor send you?"

"Hell, no! Mike would never send anyone to—" He broke off. "Sorry. No, I guess I'm just concerned."

"Then I'll tell you, in all honesty, that I don't know what I feel at all right now," Katrina said softly. "I have to figure things out myself first, okay?"

"Fair enough," he told her, standing. "Mind if I come back to see you now and then?"

"To keep probing?"

"No, 'cause you're the best-looking thing these eyes have seen in a long, long time."

"I don't believe that!" Katrina laughed. "I've just met a Navy nurse."

"Oh, Amy. Yeah, Amy's pretty. But she's old hat. Like living with a sister."

Katrina laughed, quite certain that Amy could never really be old hat to anyone. But she liked Stan, no matter what he was up to.

She raised her hands. "I promised the Navy three days, Stan. I guess I'll be here."

He smiled. "Oh! One more thing! Your brother-in-law is here. We told him you had bruised ribs from a falling palm branch, and that we're here to study flora and fauna. Okay?"

"Ah, yes, I guess so."

Lying to Frank wouldn't be easy.

Telling him the whole truth would be far worse!

Frank arrived soon after Stan left. "Hiya, kid!" he greeted her, giving her a quick hug, then looking around.

"Frank, I'm twenty-seven. You're twenty-five. I'm not the kid."

He whistled softly, dark eyes darting from the bed to the VCR. "Cushy setup. Not bad. A three-day paid vacation with everything you could want at your fingertips."

Katrina shook her head, wondering for a moment what Frank had gotten into. They'd always been close, even before she had married James. And when James had died, they'd naturally come even closer. They'd had to keep afloat together, and they'd done it very well.

"Have you been drinking?"

"Just one Scotch in the dining room, short stuff."

She hesitated just a second. "What are you doing here?"

"I was at McHennesy's getting ready to light out and make sure you and Jason had gotten through the storm okay. I came back with him to see how you were—you know Frank to the rescue! Then I learned that the Navy had already been to the rescue. A sailor to help you through the storm, and now hospital care for you both. I'm impressed—and damned glad."

She sniffed. "I'm not. This is very inconvenient."

"Why?"

"Why? Don't we have a fishing party coming up?"

"So? I can handle it."

"Are you insinuating I'm not needed?"

He laughed. "No, partner, nothing like that." His dark

eyes flashed. "You are, however, best at assuring our customers of a decorative view for the day!"

"Thanks! Hey, who's senior partner here?"

He ignored her. "And I've a new, luscious blond girlfriend who fills the bill admirably."

"Well! The hell with you!" she retorted playfully. "Besides, there's my social life that's being inconvenienced. . . ."

"What social life, Kat?" He interrupted her very softly.

"Frank, if you came to sit there and insult me . . ."

"I didn't come to insult you. I just spoke the truth. You live like a hermit." He paused. "James wouldn't have wanted that." He didn't give her a chance to reply, but continued on. "This is an interesting situation. The Navy is here, and you're getting shook up a little bit. I like it."

"Frank!" She moaned. "Go home!"

He laughed, tousling her hair. "I am going home. I just wanted to see you, short stuff."

"You've seen me! Let me suffer in peace!"

"Bye, Kat. Take care. I'll see you soon, huh? And don't worry about anything, just make sure that everything is okay. They say they're keeping Jason with you. That's great too. He loves it. Really, that they should be so concerned . . ."

"It's wonderful. Just wonderful," Katrina murmured. He frowned curiously at her reply, then kissed her forehead. "Take care. Call me as soon as you're home."

He started to leave, then paused in the doorway. "By the way, I like that Taylor guy. Jason does too."

"He's just a doll," Katrina said acidly.

Frank lifted a brow. "My, my, the Kat's got her claws bared, watch out!"

She smiled sweetly. "Frank, go home."

He grinned. "Bye."

Jason came in next, all excited. Mike, it seemed, had gotten permission from the admiral to show him all around the ship. He talked nonstop to Katrina for about half an hour.

She finally managed to ask him if he had spoken with his grandmother Matty. "Oh, she's mad. At you. Says you should have come over and talked to her too. Grandpa said that she should hush up, though. That you were a big girl."

Katrina grimaced, but decided she'd better ask for a phone and call her mother before she could call her. She talked to both her parents, swearing that she was fine, promising to see them soon. The story had already spread that the Navy was there, studying something-or-the-other. Mathilda wanted to rush over to see Katrina's "poor ribs," but Katrina's father managed to calm her down and free Katrina from the phone with a loving "We'll see you soon, kitten, as soon as it's convenient."

Then Amy came in, patient and ready to listen to Jason's nonstop excitement, too, and managed to get his blood pressure, a blood sample, a temperature, and everything else she needed from him at the same time.

Dinner came next, served on trays by the chief petty officer. Katrina and Jason managed to eat on her bed, with the trays between them.

The admiral came to say good-night and to warn her that he'd be spending a lot of time with her the next day. Then Al Stradford came by to say good-night; he was very polite and charming.

When he left, Jason went into his own bed, exhausted from the day's excitement.

Katrina lay awake a long time, burning miserably inside. What had she expected from Mike? she asked herself bitterly. And what did she want from him?

Nothing! she told herself, and in time she finally drifted to sleep.

She woke strangely, slowly, with the sensation that someone was watching her. Someone was. He was sitting in the recliner, staring at her patiently, as if he knew his presence could wake her up.

As soon as her eyes touched his, she sat up, as wary as if he were a snake. "What are you doing here?" she demanded hoarsely.

"It's the first chance I've had to come by."

"I don't want to see you. I only agreed to do this because the admiral said that he was taking charge."

"Don't worry, Mrs. Denver," he said coolly. "I'm not your doctor."

"Then why are you here?" She didn't know why she was lashing out at him so bitterly. Yes, she did. It had just been last night that she had walked into his room, last night that he had held her so tenderly and forced her to make love with her eyes open, forced her to admit her desires, enjoy them, enjoy him, and fall a little bit in love with him because of his strength and his care and his vital masculinity.

And then this morning—the terrible truth!

His sandy head bent slightly. "I wanted to tell you, too, that I've taken a leave of absence."

"What?" She frowned, and he smiled mockingly.

"Sorry, I will still be around on the island. But I asked for a leave of absence because I believe it's me you want to hang, not the entire military." He stood, and she looked away. She didn't want to watch him because she'd want to touch him. His hands, with their tapering fingers and neatly clipped nails. His shoulders, muscles occasionally straining against the white of his shirt when he moved. His eyes, with all their silver-and-steel magic. "I'll still be working, but working on my own."

"For the Navy," she murmured.

"For—and removed from. Good night, Mrs. Denver."

She rolled on her side, turning her back to him. He paused, smiling bitterly. Her hair looked like a blanket of fire against the white of the sheets. His hands itched to touch it; he wanted to shake her, to tell her that what they had was unique and beautiful, and that she had to see it.

"By the way, I'm thirty-eight—not forty."

The door closed behind him and she swung around, wincing. So Stan Thorpe had repeated their conversation together. What had she said to Stan Thorpe?

* * *

Katrina spent the morning being poked and prodded, albeit very gently, by the admiral. She was amazed by the facilities on the ship, and even more amazed to gaze out the window and see that a silver dome was rising on her island.

"That's the lab," the admiral told her. He grinned, proud of his achievements. "It will be up and functional by tonight."

Katrina was glad that no strobes were attached to her then, because she knew her heartbeat had quickened. "I understand that Captain Taylor has taken a leave of absence."

"Yes," the admiral said, and he looked at her curiously. "He seems to feel that you're angry with him, and not us. Is that so, Mrs. Denver? If you've a reason, you should let me know."

She hoped to hell that they didn't have a lie detector among the gadgets on board.

"No, no reason," she said flatly.

The admiral didn't push the point. He went in to see Jason, and Katrina bit down on her lip.

Katrina endured another day of being poked and prodded. She and Jason watched an action-adventure film on the VCR, played Go Fish and gin rummy, and ate their meals in their rooms. Jason thought that it was all great fun.

At night Stan came back to bring her tea again. He just sat awhile, joking lightly about military procedure and doctors in general. She was angry because he'd obviously repeated their previous conversation to Mike, but she really liked him and enjoyed his company.

Everyone seemed to come by, except for Michael.

Right as she turned off all her lights to fall asleep, Katrina heard voices outside her door.

"Hi, gorgeous. How's it going?" It was Mike.

"The usual. The kid is a luv. Mrs. Denver is wary, but very cooperative and pleasant."

"Jason is great."

Katrina gritted her teeth together as she heard Mike emphasizing the fact that Jason was wonderful. His omission of her was definite declaration that he thought her a witch.

"What are you doing later?"

"Nothing—I'm off at eleven."

"Stan and I are going to Marathon for drinks. Want to come?"

"Sure thing, Doc. I'll see you then."

Footsteps moved away, and Katrina seethed. He was making a date with the gorgeous nurse.

He wasn't even going to ask how she was doing!

She slammed her fist into her pillow. *Mike Taylor!* she thought. *I hope you run into another reef! I hope the sharks eat you! I hope—*

"Mrs. Denver? Are you all right?"

The beautiful nurse, kindly concerned, was standing by her bed. "Can I get you anything?"

Yes, bring me the head of Michael Taylor!

She smiled. "No, I'm sorry. I guess I'm just restless. I didn't mean to alarm you."

"I'm here to be called if you should need me," Amy protested sincerely. She smiled. "And Lucy will be on duty all night. Don't hesitate if you need a thing!"

Katrina wished her a pleasant good-night. Then she lay awake for hours, staring at the ceiling, feeling the sea move beneath her.

On the third day, just as he had promised, the admiral released her and Jason, thanking them profusely, giving them both an entirely clean bill of health, and reminding them that for the time being, they had promised to keep things confidential.

Katrina was elated to get back to her house, to freedom. The only flaw, of course, was the prefab laboratory sitting beside one of the pools: the lab where Mike Taylor would be working.

It was Friday, a week since she had met him. She decided to let Jason stay out of school for the remainder of that last day. Most of the kids had missed several days, anyway, while they had cleaned up after the storm.

She had Harry over for a barbecue. On Sunday she went into church; on Tuesday she and Frank took out a rowdy fishing party. The Navy remained just off the beach.

The admiral called her from time to time from the ship, to ask how she was doing. Stan Thorpe called her too. Al Stradford sent flowers and called.

But she didn't hear from Mike Taylor, not directly. She did get to hear about him from Jason, about all the wonderful things that he was doing in his laboratory, about the animals, the flowers.

"He lets you into the laboratory?" Katrina asked her son, suddenly furious all over again. What was the matter with the man? Hadn't he done enough harm? "I don't want you in there!"

Jason immediately gave her a belligerent look, as if she was denying him a great pleasure out of pure meanness.

He went into his room and shut the door.

Katrina paced the living room, then went to his door and tapped on it.

"Jason, please listen to me. I don't know what is going on in that lab. I—"

"He'd never hurt me! Never, never—and you know it!" Jason cried out defiantly. Then suddenly his door was thrown open, and he was staring at her with tear-filled eyes. "So he doesn't send flowers like that blond guy! He cares about you. He really cares about you! And he doesn't have to do things like send flowers—you just don't see it!"

Stunned, Katrina backed away from him.

"All you care about is those stupid, stinking flowers!"

It was the wrong side of too much. Katrina slapped him, and though she ached and hated herself after the motion—and hated the way he just pitifully stared at her—she simply turned away and walked back to the sofa. It was dark; the lights weren't on, but she didn't notice.

A minute later Jason was behind her, his arms around her neck. She pulled him around and held him to her. "Jason,

I'm sorry. I'll go to the lab tomorrow myself and see what he's doing there. If I really believe it's okay, you can go whenever you want. Just let me see what he has in there, okay?"

Jason nodded, kissed her, and went to bed.

That night Al Stradford called her and asked her out to dinner on Friday night. "There's a brand new restaurant opening."

"Yes, the Lucky Lobster. I've heard of it."

"Well?"

"I—uh—I have to see about a baby-sitter," Katrina hedged. She didn't really have a problem. On the few occasions she joined Frank or a friend for a night out, Jason slept over on Islamorada at Harry's. Harry never minded and Jason always felt as if he was getting to camp out.

She just didn't know if she wanted to go out with Al or not.

Dinner—that was the way it was supposed to be done! Get to know people gradually. Not just hop into bed. Not the way it had been with Mike Taylor.

But Al wasn't Mike Taylor, and that was why she hesitated.

Al was charming and pleasant, and there really wasn't a reason in the world that she shouldn't go to dinner with him.

"Call me back tomorrow night? I'll let you know for sure."

The next morning she brought Jason into school and returned her own little launch to the small cove by Harry's where she kept it docked. Nervously, she remembered her promise to Jason and started down the trail to the silver structure set up there.

The door was open. Katrina stood there, not going in, just waiting for her eyes to adjust to the artificial light. There was movement within, and she realized that there were cages full of possums and squirrels lining shelves along the walls. There was a table in the center of the room. The setup did remind her a little of a mad scientist's laboratory, and she had to smile.

"Just set them on the table, please."

Startled by the voice, she jumped, and she realized that just inside, to her right, Mike was sitting on a stool, staring at something through a microscope on a tall-legged desk.

She smiled a little ruefully. "I—uh—haven't got anything to put on the table."

He looked up immediately. For a single instant she thought that his eyes lit up with pleasure; but then they changed as he leaned back on the stool, watching her guardedly.

"Mrs. Denver. What a surprise."

She walked on into the room, feeling a little desperate. *Don't you remember?* she wanted to shout. *Remember that you held me and touched me, and offered a tenderness that I thought was magic?*

"What can I do for you, Mrs. Denver?" he asked her politely, very much the scientist in a white lab coat.

She stopped where she stood, about five feet from him. "I told Jason last night that he couldn't come here anymore."

"Why?"

He was suddenly on his feet, very tall, scowling darkly. Before she could think of a reply to his explosive question, he was closing the distance between them, grasping her shoulders, drawing her to him tensely.

"Damn it, Katrina, I still think your personal problem is with yourself—not me. But I can't seem to make you listen to anything I have to say. Then to go so far as to hurt the boy out of spite!"

"It's not spite!" she raged. Oh, God! Why had she bothered to come? This was worse, being held by him, feeling the heat of his body touch hers, but not his body itself.

She tried to pull away from him, but he held her too tightly.

"Captain Taylor"—Katrina gasped for breath—"try to understand. Jason was drugged! I came upon him in your arms! He might have been . . . And he's my only child! Please, this isn't spite! I just want to make sure that . . ."

Her voice trailed away. For a precious moment his body

touched hers as he pulled her close, rubbing the back of her neck intimately with gentle fingers, murmuring against the strands of her hair.

"I didn't think. . . . I'm sorry. Really sorry."

Then he pulled away from her, holding her at arm's length to smile. "Katrina, there's nothing here he can get into. Honest to God. Anything even remotely dangerous is in the locked cabinets, over there. When Jason is here, I watch him very carefully. I let him see the animals. Hold the possums—"

"Possums bite!" Katrina protested feebly.

"Not these possums!" he assured her. "Come on, I'll show you." He led her eagerly over to one of the cages, and she loved the light in his eyes when he tried to explain what he was doing. "I've tried injected doses on these guys, and I think I've got it just about right." He laughed. "No more of that awful copulating all over the place!"

She met his eyes. They both remembered the squirrels, and she blushed, then laughed, then blushed again, remembering herself.

"Anyway, see?" He opened the cage and drew out the possum. Katrina hesitated. When she had been in school, a friend had once received a nasty bite from one of them.

"Take him!"

She must have had a lot of faith in him, because she reached out for the creature. He snuggled right into her arms.

"Okay, he's agreeable now, but—"

Mike was shaking his head. "I swear, Katrina, I don't let Jason touch any of them if I'm not totally certain of their harmlessness."

She nodded, lowering her head. "Jason was—uh—very hurt. He'll be happy now, I guess."

Mike set the possum back into its cage. Then he turned to her, leaning against it, his eyes curiously cryptic.

"And what about his mother?"

"I don't know what you mean."

"Don't you?"

His hand came to her face, his palm cupping her chin, his thumb stroking her cheek. She couldn't move, could only stare at him, fascinated by his gesture, by the touch she lived with in her dreams each night, but could no longer accept.

What did he really want from her? she wondered achingly, and in a second she knew. Because his head bent and his lips touched hers, and before she knew what she was doing, she was fused with him, like a moth to flame, sighing deep in her throat. She leaned easily against his chest, feathered the hair at his nape through her fingers, savored in sweet mindlessness the mercurial heat of his tongue, giving her body a new pulse.

This was where she wanted to be, against his heartbeat, against the power and strength and warmth of him, held and cherished and loved. . . .

Unbidden, the memory of his words to Amy in the hallway came to her mind. "Hi, gorgeous!" Was Amy one of his conquests? And, oh, God, hadn't she herself been the easiest conquest of all?

His hand was on her, familiarly, possessively. Firm, moving around her hip, caressing her breast . . .

"No!"

She broke away from him, turning her back to him. Even then she felt him stiffen.

"All right, Katrina. Hang me. Hang me because you're a coward. Run. Cocoon yourself in the island. Go ahead. Hate me because you've discovered that you're not a saint, that you want me."

It was so close to the truth. She swung around defiantly. "Wrong, Captain. I don't live in a cocoon. I'm rather aware of the world. I do, in fact, have a date for Friday night."

"With who?" His eyes narrowed sharply as he stepped forward, grasping her wrist. She tried to free herself and failed, and so stared up at him. "Al Stradford. Now let me go!"

"Don't go out with him," Mike said tensely.

"Why ever not? I like his style. And he asked me out to dinner, not to bed."

"I hadn't realized that I was dealing with a woman who could be bought."

"Speak for yourself, Captain. You're the one who's been attempting to buy me, attempting to buy my silence!"

"Oh, for God's sake, sue me! Let's get past it! Then we can get on to you, lady. I'm not afraid; you are."

"Let me go."

"Oh, I am. Right now. But I'm going to ask you one more time, Katrina—don't go with him."

She tossed her head back. "Why? Because of your rivalry? Is there nothing else to gamble or bet on but who will she and who will she not go out with? Well, sorry, Taylor, I find him charming. You lost this one."

He shook his head slowly. "I'll be damned if I'll lose this one, Katrina. You don't even know what the stakes are." He let go of her arm, smiled grimly, and indicated the door.

"There you go. Freedom. Just be very careful with it, Katrina. And bear this in mind: When it's over, I promise that I will be the winner. I gamble very, very carefully."

She didn't understand him at all. All that she saw was the silver threat in his eyes, and the open door.

And his hand, indicating it.

She fled, wondering how his touch could be such magic.

And the lack of it such an utter hell.

CHAPTER NINE

Jason was at Harry's, Al had been charming so far, yet Katrina was still feeling a chill of panic. What in God's name was she doing out with the man?

The problem was that she knew the answer; she was out to spite Michael Taylor, and it was really a sorry reason. At the bar with Al she ordered a vodka martini, then wondered why she had; she could barely sip the things. When they were seated, she ordered another.

He took her hand once their drinks were served. She managed not to wrench it away, grateful when the waitress came for their orders. They decided to start with conch chowder and conch fritters, then share the red snapper and the grouper.

"If a restaurant is going to make it in the Keys," Katrina told Al teasingly, finally retrieving her hand, "it has to do a good job with grouper, snapper, and conch!"

He chuckled, then told her which fish to order in various parts of the world. She asked him about the places he had been, and in turn, he asked her about the groups she took out to the reefs for diving and snorkeling. It was easy, very easy.

Until Katrina felt a tap on her shoulder and turned around to see her mother-in-law standing behind her.

"Oh!" she gasped out, and the color instantly bled from her face, though she couldn't have said exactly why. Nancy Denver was smiling very pleasantly, happy as always to see her.

"Mom!" Katrina cried, hopping to her feet. She embraced

the older woman, then remembered that she had an introduction to make.

"Mom, this is Captain Al Stradford of the Navy. Al, this is my mother-in-law, Nancy Denver."

As always, Al was perfectly circumspect, standing, offering Nancy a seat, making all the proper remarks.

"Would you like a drink, Mrs. Denver?" Al asked.

"No, Captain, thank you." She smiled at Katrina, and Katrina felt a bit like dying. Her mother-in-law was still such a lovely woman, tall and thin as James had been, with beautiful, clean-cut features and huge dark eyes that never failed to remind Katrina of both her husband and her son. Except that Nancy's eyes carried a hint of tragedy; one that would never go away. Being a mother, Katrina understood. A woman could never, never lose a child and learn to come to terms with it completely.

"Dad's at the bar. I think our table is about ready."

"You're welcome to join us!" Katrina said quickly. Did Al's eyes narrow a bit with displeasure at her invitation? Katrina wasn't sure, and though it was rude, she really didn't care. She suddenly felt horrible, as if she had been caught playing with matches as a child. Yet Nancy wasn't acting that way; she was behaving as if it were perfectly normal to run into Katrina on a date.

She shook her head. "Thanks, dear, but no thanks. We're here with Frank and a friend of his. How's Jason?"

"Fine, Mom. Anxious to see you. As soon as the Navy—"

Nancy smiled at Al. "Yes, dear. I'd heard you had some Navy men there, studying wildlife, is it?"

"Yes!" Katrina said quickly.

"Captain, I hope you won't mind if Katrina brings you by our table later. My husband will be awfully disappointed if he doesn't get a chance to say hello."

Al was on his feet, perfectly polite, as soon as Nancy rose. "Of course, Mrs. Denver. It will be a pleasure to meet your husband."

Nancy smiled and gave Katrina a little wave and moved back into the crowd.

"She's a lovely woman," Al said.

"Yes, she is," Katrina replied. And she tried very hard to smile. After all, Al hadn't done a thing wrong. Not a damn thing. But Katrina was miserable. She wanted to rush to her mother-in-law and cry out that it was only dinner, only dinner.

With this man, yes, it was only dinner. But there was another man with whom it had been much, much more.

She promptly ordered another martini.

"I think Toni's planning on a medical career," Mike told Amy, who had wisely brought up the subject of his only offspring to keep his mind occupied. Amy and Mike were old friends; he'd told her the truth about the evening. Al had told Stan where he was taking Katrina; Stan had told Mike. Mike had decided to keep an eye on the pair, and with a weary sigh, Amy had agreed to accompany him. "Toni is a good kid, she'll do well," Amy told Mike, sipping her champagne. Her eyes narrowed; Mike had turned as red as a beet.

"Hey—your eyes are about to fall out, Captain. Get them nonchalantly back into your head and tell me what's happening."

"That's her mother-in-law Stradford is meeting!"

Amy laughed. "How in hell can you know that?"

"Because I've seen her picture," Mike murmured distractedly. God, he felt like a kid again! All tied up in knots inside because Al Stradford had met someone close to her before he'd had a chance to himself!

"So, he's meeting her mother-in-law. Mike, a lot of people probably know her mother-in-law," Amy said logically. "Pay attention to your food. You don't want them to see you gaping, do you?"

Neither of them had seen them at all yet, Mike thought with a certain annoyance; he had bribed the maître d' for a booth in the back just so that they wouldn't be seen. Yet if Katrina had ever bothered to look up, she could have seen them. She didn't look up, though. She was too busy laughing at Al's witty little quips.

"Frank's here," he said suddenly, catching sight of Jason's uncle. "Come on." He was reaching across the table for Amy's hand.

"Michael!" Amy wailed. "If you embarrass me—"

"I won't embarrass you, I swear!"

He led Amy through the crowded tables to a foursome in the middle of the floor.

"Excuse me, Frank. I saw you all come in, and just thought that we should come over and say hello."

"Mike!" Frank, with his pleasant smile and easygoing manner, was quickly on his feet. Mike introduced Amy, and in return met Frank's pretty blond friend, and Nancy and Ted Denver. Ted Denver, like his wife, was tall and slim, with intelligent, hazel eyes.

They exchanged pleasantries, then Nancy Denver said softly, "Jason is quite fond of you, Captain."

"That's good to hear. He's a fine boy, and I admit to being rather fond of him too. Well, excuse us again. We didn't mean to interrupt your dinner."

"No interruption at all," Ted said. "Thank you, Captain. I appreciate your coming over. Amy, it was our pleasure."

Amy smiled; Mike started to lead her back through the tables. "Be seeing you, Captain!" Frank called after him.

"You're after the girl—not her in-laws!" Amy reminded him when they were seated.

Mike lifted his drink to her. "But it never hurts to have popular opinion in your favor!"

Amy laughed. "Okay, you old heartbreaker. I have to admit I am enjoying this! Michael Taylor—in love at last. Down on earth with the rest of us!"

A fleeting glimpse of pain passed through his eyes, and Amy, who knew him so well, was sorry for her glib words. She knew he was thinking about Margo. "In love at last—again," he murmured, his voice a touch bitter.

Her fingers curled around his strong ones where they lay on the table. "Hey, Captain! I'm in your corner!"

And he smiled. "Thanks."

It was as Mike was talking to her father-in-law that Katrina at last saw him. A conch fritter stuck in her throat; she coughed, drained her third martini, then coughed all over again.

He wasn't alone! He was with Amy, the tall, slim, beautiful brunette nurse. Oh! So some people he invited to dinner—and some people he just rolled in the sand!

And he had the nerve—the gall!—to stand there talking with the Denvers, laughing with Frank! And Frank, damn him to hell, was laughing back, calling out to him as he led the pretty, pretty brunette back to their dimly lit booth.

"Another drink, Katrina?"

The brunette was reaching across the table, covering his hand with her elegant, lovely, long-nailed fingers.

"Yes! I mean, please."

"You haven't finished your fish. Isn't it okay?"

She smiled weakly. "Oh, no, the fish is fine."

She was still staring over his shoulder. And all of a sudden Mike Taylor was staring at her across the crowded restaurant. Their eyes met—and clashed. He was looking at her as if she were a stubborn, bratty child, and as if someone ought to take a hickory stick to her. As if he would like to be that someone.

Oh! She narrowed her eyes, and glared back at him. And when her martini arrived, she picked it up and swallowed it in one gulp, still so busy glaring at him that she didn't realize this fourth drink had hit her like a ton of bricks.

He stared a second longer. Then his eyes left hers.

"It's getting warm in here, don't you think?" Al asked her. She didn't notice his curious expression. "Want to take a little walk by the water? There's a patio outside—we can come back for coffee, if you like."

"Ah . . . yes! Yes, it's very warm."

Mike's eyes were on her again. He'd actually looked past his date to raise his glass to her, his expression totally mocking.

She ignored him and smiled radiantly at Al, practically purring.

"I'd love to take a walk!"

She remembered then—with a very guilty conscience—to say hello to her father-in-law. Except that it wasn't that easy. The martinis had definitely hit her. Even standing was an effort. Concentrating very hard, she made her way carefully to their table. Ted's hug almost knocked her over. She said hello to Connie, Frank's friend, then started back to her own table.

But Frank caught her halfway there.

"Katrina!"

"What?"

"You're—you're loaded!"

"I am not!" she protested, then leaned closer to him. "Oh, Frank! I didn't do anything wrong in front of your parents, did I?"

He shook his head impatiently. "No, no. You're acting just fine. It's just that you don't drink, and I can see it in your eyes. And I can see in his eyes"—he indicated Al over her shoulder—"that you're out with a wolf on the prowl."

"Al? Oh, pooh, Frank! You're the one befriending the wolf!"

Frank chuckled. "Mike Taylor? Yeah, I like him. That's beside the point. The point—"

"Frank!" Katrina pleaded. "I'm twenty-seven! I can take care of myself!"

"I know. Just be careful, and don't you dare have another drink!"

"I won't," Katrina assured him miserably. She could see two of him swaying before her.

"I love you, kid," he told her.

"I love you too. And you're the kid!"

He shook his head sadly and released her. But after he watched her walk out of the building with Stradford, he didn't return to his seat. He walked on down to the booth that Mike and Amy were sharing and slid in beside Amy.

"Excuse me!" He flashed Amy one of his most charming smiles.

She laughed. "Go right ahead. I'm just along for the ride!"

Frank leaned across the table to talk to Mike. "I think

that my sister-in-law is tipsy if not downright inebriated. And your friend looks like the cat about to swallow the canary. I can go after her, but she'd die if my parents became involved."

Mike was already up, tossing money on the table, reaching for Amy's hand. "Let's go neck."

"I will not!"

"Fake it, then?"

"Oh, what the hell!" Amy moaned. "I've had dinner—I guess it's time for some entertainment."

Even as Katrina walked hand in hand with Al down the boardwalk that paralleled the water, she knew that Mike was gone from his booth. She could see that it was empty.

As they went farther and farther away, toward darkness and foliage, she became aware that down beneath the moonlight, Mike and Amy were out for a stroll too.

Jealousy streaked through her like a bitter, bitter gall. She stumbled in her heels against the wooden walk, and when Al swept an arm around her to support her, she fell against him. And laughed. And when he leaned her against the rail, arms on either side of her, she laughed again, setting her hands against his chest.

It was probably very natural that he should kiss her, and natural that he should be pretty expert at his task, stripping away her defenses quickly with a firm, roving tongue. Yet she felt that she was outside of herself, completely removed, watching someone else. And all she could think was that he really wasn't touching her at all. She didn't feel anything: no thrill of passion, no wonderful heat to dance and ripple along her spine, no urge to touch him, to know his touch any further. All she felt was dizzy, and crushed, and too warm.

Then, quite suddenly, she couldn't be outside of herself anymore. Because he was an expert, and his arms were about her, sweeping her around, down from the sandy plain to a place shrouded in darkness and palms. And she was on her back, and he was above her; he was kissing her still, but his hands—my God! Did he have ten of them? Every time she tried to combat him, he was someplace else. And she couldn't breathe! Her head was spinning so badly. Her skirt was hiked halfway up to her waist and his thumb was on her breast, bare beneath the light material.

At last she managed to twist her lips from his, to cry out against him.

"Al! Stop—"

"Ah, baby, come on! You were leaning against me, kissing me back, asking for some action all night!"

"No—"

His mouth covered hers, a panic reached her through the dull, throbbing haze of the vodka. She tried to kick him from her, and received his touch along her inner thigh. She realized then with frightening clarity that she was a ninety-nine-pound woman and he was a husky, well-muscled man. And that she had carelessly gotten herself into a horrible position. But, dear God, he couldn't mean to rape her, right here, outside of the restaurant.

"No!" she cried again.

"Katrina, no one can see us."

"No!"

His mouth ground against hers, and she wasn't at all sure of his intentions anymore. He was grasping at her pantyhose, his hand on her hip.

"No—ohh!"

He was suddenly gone, so suddenly that she lay stunned, desperately trying to smooth her clothing decently back around her body. She was trying to sit up, trying to decipher what had happened.

And then she knew; not five feet away, two men were tousling in the sand. She heard the sickening crunch of blows, gutteral threats.

Mike Taylor had wrenched Al from her.

Another blow sounded, then a splash as someone landed in the water. Then words again.

"She's my date, Taylor! What's the matter—can't get your own?"

"She said no, Stradford!"

"She said no to you, Taylor; that's the problem, isn't it? She was asking for it—from *me!*"

And then Mike spoke again, saying words that humiliated her to the core. "All right, Stradford. She was a flirt. Egging you on. But she didn't want it as far as you did, so that's where it's got to end."

"What are you, her guardian angel? Responsible for her?"

"Yeah, responsible."

Another blow fell. Katrina closed her eyes in absolute misery. She opened them again and found a slim hand outstretched to her. It was the brunette nurse, Amy.

She stared at the hand. "Oh, dear God!" she murmured miserably. "Look at what, at what I—one of them is going to hurt the other."

Miraculously, Amy laughed. "No, Mrs. Denver, let them be. This has been coming on for years. It really isn't your fault. They're both enjoying every second of it."

Thanks to Amy, Katrina made it to her feet. But it seemed that the nightmare was only beginning. The sound of running footsteps came down the boardwalk.

"Trina! Katrina!" Frank stopped short, right in front of her. He breathed deeply with relief. "You're all right."

Then there was a woman's voice. "Katrina! Oh, goodness! What is going on here?"

"I—"

Frank took his mother's arm. Too late—she had already seen the two men knocking it out in the surf and the sand.

Katrina wanted to die. At the very least she wanted to sink into the sand forever and ever as her mother-in-law stared at her with concerned, and very confused, eyes.

"Ma! It's all right!" Frank assured her. "Let's get out of here before Dad shows up!"

He was leading her away, but she cast a look back. "Katrina?"

Katrina had to find her voice, and she was very grateful when Amy answered for her. "We're fine, Mrs. Denver! You know boys—they have to play now and then!"

And Katrina managed a weak, weak smile. "I'll see you soon, Mom!"

"I think that I want to die!" Katrina murmured when they were gone.

"Don't be silly! After you get through your hangover, you'll be fine," Amy assured her. "Oh—I think we have a victor!"

And they did. Mike—with a bleeding lip and the promise of a black eye—was coming toward them. His mouth was dead grim, so tight it was whiter than the sand. His face was stretched taut, making his jaw a concrete square. And his eyes, piercing through Katrina with such rage, might have been steel blades.

He gripped her arm, pulling her forcibly from Amy.

"Let's go!" he growled.

She hung back, frightened. She was determined not to go anywhere with him when he looked like that.

"No! I—uh—can't. Ah, Al—"

"Don't you dare say anything right now, lady. And don't you dare give me one bit of trouble!"

"But—"

He ignored her, looking at Amy.

"Amy?"

"Oh, yeah, sure. I'll go patch him up and get him back to the ship. What's a good nurse for?"

"Thanks, Amy."

"No problem. Except that the admiral is going to skin you both for breakfast, you know!"

"Not much I can do about that," Mike murmured. His voice lowered to a furious grate as his fingers tightened around Katrina's arms. "Let's go. *Now,* Mrs. Denver."

She wanted to grasp onto the rail, but she had the sinking feeling that he would just break it off. She looked at Amy, allowing her to see the naked plea in her eyes.

But nothing much seemed to faze Amy.

"Don't worry!" she told Katrina cheerfully. "His growl is ten times worse than his bite!"

No help there.

And then Mike's whisper was touching her ear, warm and staccato and tense.

"Want to walk—or be carried?"

She started walking. But in the end, after they had skirted the restaurant and reached the dock, he picked her up after all. Her heel had caught in a plank, and the vodka had so dazed her reflexes that she almost fell.

Not that he carried her gently. He swung her into his arms roughly, then practically tossed her into the rear of a dinghy.

She didn't move. She closed her eyes, vowing that she never wanted to even see a bottle of vodka again, and prayed that Michael Taylor and the entire night might disappear when she opened her eyes again.

But he was still there, his expression masked by the night as the dinghy streaked out into the water.

CHAPTER TEN

The breeze felt good, almost as good as the salt spray that licked Katrina's face as the launch moved through the night. She had been born by the seaside, had learned to swim before she had walked, and spent her entire life with boats.

She'd never been seasick in her life. She felt like absolute hell now, tempted beyond all measure to throw herself over the side of the speeding launch.

She didn't move. She didn't like Mike's shadowed expression, not one bit. She didn't want to think of herself as being a coward, but at this moment she was. What a mess! Al, back there somewhere in the sand. Mike, furious. Nancy Denver having come upon the whole scene. Oh, God! How could she have hurt her mother-in-law so?

"Oh, you macho idiot!" she suddenly raged. "It was your fault! The whole damn, humiliating thing was your fault!"

The tail end of her shout filled her ears like ringing bells; she hadn't realized that they were so close to the island, and Mike had cut the motor.

"My fault?" he said in a deathly quiet voice.

The dinghy scraped bottom. He leapt past her, landing neatly in the damp sand, pulling the dinghy high onto it before reaching out a hand to help her from it. She didn't want to take that hand; she wasn't given a chance to refuse. She was suddenly standing on the sand, sand that swayed miserably beneath the moonlight. Out on the water she could see the Navy cutter, alive with light. The island seemed to offer only darkness, but the darkness didn't relieve her mind, it just swayed along with the sand.

He dragged her along at a furious pace. One of her heels caught, and she cried out, staggered by the pain in her ankle.

He swung around to pick her up, and she instantly wished that she were a larger woman, so that she couldn't be tossed about so easily—like baggage!

"Let me down, I can walk!" She pitted a blow against his chest; his eyes didn't even fall to hers.

In another minute they were at the house. He knew she never locked her door; it slammed and reverberated when he closed it behind them. She found herself gracelessly set on the couch, her skirt riding too high, her feet a tangle beneath her. She scurried to rectify her position, but it didn't matter; he wasn't looking at her. He was pacing the floor behind her, one set of fingers threading through his hair, the other white-knuckled in a grip on his hip.

"My fault? My fault, Mrs. Denver?"

His eyes were on her again; she decided that she had been much better off when he had been staring distractedly at the walls.

"Yes!" she flared. "You bastard! If you hadn't been there—"

"If I hadn't been there, you'd have been raped. Oh, excuse me—unless you were egging him on purposely?"

Even through her haze of pain it was too much. She muttered a curse that told him exactly what he should do with himself, slamming both her fists against the chest that prevented her escape.

He captured her wrists and sat at her side, the bite of his fingers like steel around her, his wrath increasing so that he leaned again, forcing her back into the soft cushions of the sofa.

"I'm more than willing to be corrected if I'm wrong, Mrs. Denver!" he told her angrily. "Please, do tell me! Did I interrupt the high point of your evening? *How was I at fault?"*

By being there! she wanted to scream. *By being there with a tall and beautiful brunette! By wrenching me apart. . . .*

But she couldn't say that.

"Where on God's earth do you get off being so righteous!"

she cried, tears stinging her eyes. "So Al Stradford was using muscle! So—"

"For God's sake, he was going to use you, nothing more!"

"And where is that any less than what you did? You and your damned drugs!"

He released her, so abruptly that she sank into the soft cushions on the sofa. And then he was standing again, pacing behind the sofa. She scrambled to sit up, but she was too late. He was behind her, his fingers curling over her bare shoulders, the heat of his mocking whisper feathering onto her shoulders.

"My drug, Mrs. Denver? Is that what it was in this house, the night you walked into my bedroom?"

A little wildly she began to babble. "Your bedroom! You forget this is my house! My house, my island! Mine! And you invaded the island, the house—and me! So I ask you again, what was your problem with Al?"

To her horror she started to laugh, heedless of the bite of his fingers against her shoulders. "But then, that wasn't really over me tonight anyway, was it? That was just a fight that had been brooding between the two of you for years! I was just a damned convenient excuse, and nothing more!"

"Don't be more of a fool than you've already made yourself out to be!"

"What is it to you? Can't you just please, please leave me alone?" A sob suddenly choked against her throat as she remembered Nancy Denver's expression of anxiety and concern.

Katrina buried her face in her hands, totally heedless of his touch as she groaned. "Nancy saw the whole damn thing. Oh, God!"

"She could have seen you with Al. Half undressed. Or before, when you were exercising your lips with such finesse!"

"I hate you!" She swung at him, to little avail. He clutched her hands again, leapt over the couch, and pinned her back down to it.

"Will you quit, Katrina!"

"Will you just get out of here, please?"

She couldn't bear the pressure of his hard body against her, the vise of his fingers, the scent of him, his flesh, brushing hers. Memories were evoked too easily, memories of those strong, tapered fingers moving upon her with gentleness, stroking her needs to flame, making her feel so vital and alive.

She twisted her head, her eyes burning again with the promise of tears.

"Please!" she begged him again in a husky whisper. "Oh, God, what is the difference? You, Al, or the whole damn fleet!"

She'd meant to anger him, to send him away. She was startled by his silence, by the easing of his fingers around her wrists. Still, his chest was against hers; her slim legs were entangled with his. She could feel his muscles, sinew by sinew, honed and taut and wired with emotion.

His hand caught her cheek, drew her eyes to his. He studied her long and hard, until she ached with wonder, wanted to scream and demand to know what he found in his assessment. She wanted so very badly for him to release her so that she could run, hide, bury her face into her pillow, ease the humiliation and misery of the evening.

"There's a tremendous difference," he said suddenly. "I'm going to marry you."

"Why, Captain? Because a wife can't testify against her husband in court—or something like that? To keep me from spewing your precious experiments all over the newspapers? Forget it, Captain. I've been married. Really married. You egotist!"

And then the tears that she had fought so strenuously to hold back spilled forth, streaming down her cheeks. "You are not James! You're nothing like him! And I—"

"You're doing your damn best to live in his grave with him, Katrina, but it just doesn't work and you just can't stand it. But where is your problem, then? You're so worried about everyone's opinion! Marry me. Sure—we solve my problems. And we solve yours. No more teasing, overzealous men—you can get what you want right at home, no recriminations from the world. It's a sorry thing to have to admit, Katrina, isn't it? But you are human. You can't live either on a pedestal or in a grave."

"Let me up! Get out of here! I don't want—"

She stopped suddenly, aware that the vodka and the little bit of dinner that she had consumed were warring in her stomach

She stared at him, pitiably. "Oh, God, please! Let me up!"

Warily, but touched by the sincerity of her plea and the ghostly white pallor of her complexion, Mike moved. Katrina bolted up, raced into her bathroom, and was violently sick.

Shaking, trembling, barely able to stand, she washed her face and furiously brushed her teeth.

He was banging on the door. She stared at her white face with its huge blue-green eyes in the mirror above the sink. She was going to start crying all over again. All she wanted to do was pass out and forget the night.

"Katrina!"

"Go away!" she faltered out, and she gripped the sink, holding on to it tightly.

There was a shuddering sound; had she locked the door to her bedroom, and had he broken it? Or had he just opened it with such force that it had sounded that way?

It didn't matter; her head was spinning and he was suddenly standing in the bathroom doorway, frowning intensely.

"You're sick?"

The query made her feel like laughing—or crying.

"No," she retorted. "I feel like running the Boston Marathon."

He started to walk toward her; she lifted up with horror a weakly defensive hand. "Oh, please! Can't you just go away?"

His reaction then startled her, so much so that she couldn't even protest his touch when his arms came gently around her.

"No, I can't go away."

He eased her around, making her sit on the toilet. Then he turned on the water in the bathtub.

"What are you doing?"

"You can climb into the bathtub and soak a little of it out while I fix some juice and coffee."

"No."

"Trust me, you'll be glad in the morning."

"You told me to trust you once before! And I'm not—I'm not getting into that tub with you here!"

"I don't take advantage of innocents—or seductresses, whichever you choose to be for the moment. Come on let me help you."

"No," she protested, but to no avail. He was on his knees beside her, stripping away her shoes, hiking her weight against him to slide his fingers up to the top of her pantyhose.

"Please!" She was almost in tears again. "I don't want your help. I can help—"

Her voice muffled away as he pulled her dress over her shoulders. She sat there, shaking and bare and miserable, while he checked the warmth of the water.

"Mrs. Denver," he said softly, his back to her, "I do believe that you can help yourself. But sometimes it's just not necessary."

He turned around, and she instantly hunched her shoulders, causing him to laugh. "Katrina, I've memorized every inch of you. Every inch. And I swear, I'm not about to take advantage of you now."

"Now!" she retorted, eyes downcast. "So you admit that you did before!"

"Oh, let a dead dog lie, will you?"

She had little choice; the next sound she issued was a gasp as his arms wrapped around her naked flesh. But she didn't feel his searing touch for long; he very carefully deposited her in the tub, catching the length of her hair dexterously before it could hit the water, winding it into a knot above her head.

She brought her knees to her chest and wrapped her arms around them swiftly, afraid to admit that the warmth of the water had already enveloped her, made her feel much, much better.

Inadvertently, she stared at his face while he finished securing her hair. And once again she felt the urge to cry. No, he wasn't James. But he was so very strong and assured and competent, sometimes hard, sometimes so tender. Rugged planes, lean features, determination, handsome, sensual lips, and silver eyes that could both pierce and caress.

It was disloyal to love . . . but she did love him, and it was terrifying.

His eyes caught hers, so tremulous on his own. "Don't drown on me!" he warned her softly; then he was up. At the doorway he paused, frowning again.

"Where's Jason?"

"At—at Harry's," she murmured. "Spending the night. Harry will bring him back early."

"Good," he muttered, and was gone.

She allowed the steam to envelop her; she tried not to think, and not to feel. Not on the inside, anyway. She tried just to let the water soothe away the pounding in her head, and in her heart.

And then he was back, ready with one of her massive towels, wrapping it around her as he lifted her from the tub, not setting her down, but carrying her straight into the kitchen, and even then, holding her on his lap as he produced a glass of something red with a pair of aspirins.

"You can put me down."

"Swallow."

She did, sipping his red concoction. There was tomato juice in it, and something else. She wasn't sure that she wanted to know what else, so she didn't ask.

"Drink the whole thing."

She did, but then accused him weakly, "I know. You're trying to poison me into silence!"

He shook his head, grinning a little wistfully. "No."

He took the glass from her fingers and set it on the

counter. She was so tired now; she couldn't help but rest her head against his chest, couldn't help but appreciate the gentle feel of his fingers massaging her nape, her head.

It seemed that he sighed softly, or was it only a ripple of breeze? It didn't really matter much. She was just so tired—tired, and suddenly content, comfortable, and secure.

"Katrina?" He was calling her from a long way off. She murmured something, curling closer to his chest.

"I'm going to get you into bed."

She didn't even have a rejoinder for him; she just wanted to sleep, as sweetly comfortable as she was.

She felt as if she were floating on air. But she wasn't, of course. His arms were around her; she felt their steel.

She opened her eyes and felt his gaze so intently that she quickly allowed her lashes to flutter down once again.

Something soft greeted her; her bed. His warmth was gone; she clenched her pillow, but then he was sitting beside her, and she tried to close her mind to him once again.

He was massaging her back, absently, but his fingers felt so good. They eased away the last of her pain; she felt that she had never been cramped and miserable and sick.

He looked down at her, down at the fine lines of her profile against the pillow, the sweep of lashes. The wild mass of fire-colored hair tangled out all around her. Something inside of him quickened, and he wondered himself just what it was about one woman, one special woman, to so effect a man. To make him feel more than laughter, more than tears, more than love. To move a heart, lost in itself, and touch again so deeply all the finest things he thought that he had buried.

There was no rhyme or reason; in defeat, he made the admission. He just knew that he did love her, that he wanted to be with her, to share with her all that life might bring their way.

"Katrina . . ." His forehead knotted in a frown as he searched for the words. "Katrina, you can't play with the Al Stradfords of this world. All right, maybe I did use you; maybe what I did was even worse—"

"Ummmm . . ." she mumbled out.

He closed his eyes, squeezing his temples fiercely between his fingers. "But, Katrina, I never meant to hurt you, so help me. I never meant to use you. Katrina, I love you."

She didn't respond. He pulled his hands from his head and twisted around to view her again.

"Katrina?" He shook her slightly; all she did was clench more tightly to her pillow and sigh softly.

Oh, hell! His great confession—and she'd slept right through it. He shook his head; and then had to laugh at himself.

He rose and pulled the covers tightly around her. He paused, very tenderly kissing the top of her head, and then, whimsically, the tips of her limp fingers.

"I do love you, babe," he said very softly, then left her.

When Katrina awakened, her head was pounding like a set of hammers against twin anvils. With a great effort she opened her eyes, trying to force them into focus.

Jason was standing at the foot of her bed.

"Oh!" she cried, sitting up; then, realizing that she was undressed, pulling the covers to her chest. "Oh, Jason! I'm sorry; I overslept. School! Did you eat? I'll make your lunch; we'll get going."

"Mom!" Jason shook his head, frowning. "It's Saturday."

"Oh." She let her head crash back to the pillow.

"Mom?" She felt a shift in the bed and knew that Jason had perched worriedly by her side. "Can I get you anything? Want some water, an aspirin?"

"I—"

"Good morning!"

The next voice that accosted her was anything but gentle. It was disgustingly, sickeningly cheerful, and all the worse because it belonged to her brother-in-law.

She groaned deeply and burrowed beneath the sheets, letting out a miserable "Frank! What are you doing here?"

More weight plopped onto the other side of the bed. He tugged lightly at the sheet, bringing it down just below her eyes. His own were darkly mischievous, causing her a moment's heartache, so like James's they were.

"Trina, you look quite pathetic."

"Thank you kindly, brother dear!" she retorted. Her own voice hurt her head. "Oh, God! What did I do to deserve you this morning?"

"Hey, that's unkind! But I assume that you're paying for a multitude of sins. I thought you might want to sleep this morning."

"So you woke me up."

"No, so I came by to take my favorite nephew fishing."

"Don't let him flatter you, Jason. You're his only nephew."

"Can I go, Mom?" Jason asked excitedly.

"Yes."

"Thanks!" She felt Jason's kiss. "I'll go throw a few things in the ice chest, Uncle Frank!"

"You do that, sport!"

Frank hadn't moved. Slowly, carefully, Katrina opened her eyes. His still carried a hint of deviltry, but there was empathy in them, too, so much so that her eyes quickly filled with tears.

"Oh, Frank!"

"Hey! It's not that bad!" he told her softly. "Your headache will go away."

"It's not that. It's your mother, Frank! Oh, she saw everything that was going on. What must she have thought?"

"Katrina! If my mother felt anything, it was concern for you."

"Concern! No, no! I hurt her, Frank. I—"

"Trina, my mother loved James. With all her heart. She'll never forget him. But she loves you too. She thinks the world of you, and she has since you were a little kid. Katrina, I loved James too. With all my heart. He was my older brother, my idol, the sun, the stars, and the moon all rolled into one. Katrina, I'd admit, if you'd have run off like a spark a month after he died—or even a year—I'd have resented it. But, Kat, in October it will have been five years.

That's a long time to be alone, to live like a cloistered nun." He shook his head, searching for words. "Katrina, don't you see? You're not just an appendage of James to any of us! Not to Dad, not to Mom, not to me. We care about you. And we want you to be happy."

She groaned softly. "Last night didn't make me happy. It made me sick and miserable."

Frank chuckled softly. "Yeah, well, you do deserve it. What were you doing, wolfing down martinis like there was no tomorrow? You scared me silly." He lightly chucked her sheet-covered chin with his knuckles and grew more serious. "Don't get me wrong, Katrina. I have a sense of brotherly protectiveness you won't shake easily. That's why I dragged Mike Taylor out when you disappeared with Mr. Charisma."

Startled, Katrina twisted to stare at him. "You! No! He was out with that brunette." She paused, flinching, remembering how kind Amy had been to her. "He was on a date himself."

"Oh, not really," Frank said cryptically. He kissed her forehead. "I'm going. Get some more sleep."

He straightened; she gripped his hand suddenly. "Thanks, Frank. I love you."

"Love you too." He gave her hand a squeeze. A second later the living-room door slammed shut; she winced and closed her eyes again, relieved. But sleep wouldn't come to her; eventually she rose and made herself coffee and miserably sipped it.

Impatient with herself, Katrina slipped on a bathing suit and cover-up, grabbed her mask and fins, and headed for the beach. The reef might well be her salvation.

Her footsteps wavered as she walked past the pool and Mike's lab. But there was no sign of life there, and she hurried on by.

Katrina stepped out into the water. She rinsed her mask and secured it to her head. She slipped into her flippers and swam out to the reef.

It was just what she wanted: peace and serenity, fan coral

waving in its ghostly dance, brilliant yellow tangs darting around it. A big, ugly grouper passed her, eying her curiously. Far below her, hugging a sand spit, a manta cast its glorious body along with graceful ease. She heard only her own breath, a wind that passed through the snorkel.

It was a beautiful world, but a treacherous one too. It had taken James from her.

Yet she hadn't turned away from the island or the reefs. Why had she turned away from life?

Something snagged at her flipper. Startled, Katrina swung around. Mike was behind her.

She surfaced, ripping her mask from her head and treading water. He rose beside her, tearing his own mask away.

"What are you doing out here?" she cried out, angry and defensive, and not at all ready for another battle of wits.

"Looking for you," he told her bluntly. "I wanted to see how you were."

"I'm fine. I just—I just want to be alone!"

His features, well defined with his hair sleeked back, grew tight. "Ah, yes, the solitary Mrs. Denver!"

"If you'd just leave—"

"Leave you alone? Sorry. I'm a believer in lost causes. I like a challenge. The more you fight me, Mrs. Denver, the more I'll be around. I'm a sore loser."

"And what are you expecting to win, Captain?" she retorted.

"Why, the spoils, of course, that which the victor is always supposed to take."

Katrina slipped her mask back into place. "Captain, there isn't anything you haven't already had. Now, if you'll excuse me?"

She started back to the shore.

He followed.

She didn't know why she was so determined to lose him, but it was a feeling that was a little bit desperate. She didn't head for the beach; she headed for the mangrove roots to the north of it. Reaching them, she crawled carefully among them, sometimes in the water, sometimes out of it.

But he caught her anyway, so suddenly that his hold unbalanced her and she fell into a foot of water between two long roots.

And before she could get up, he was next to her, locking one long muscular leg over her lower torso, bracing her waist with an immovable arm.

"What do you want?" she demanded, her heart sinking. Surely he could feel the tension in her, see the pulse that beat so furiously in her throat, sense his effect upon her.

He smiled, very slowly and languorously.

"I came to see how you were feeling about my proposal."

"What proposal?"

"My marriage proposal."

She laughed nervously. "I barely know you. And I'm not at all sure I like what I know."

"I beg to differ. You know me very well. And you damned well liked every bit of getting to know me."

She hissed out something inarticulate, but her attempt to escape his hold was fruitless.

"I thought you were against brute force."

"Only when it's some other brute."

"Why are you making a mockery out of—"

"Marriage? I intend no mockery."

She started to laugh again, determined to be as hard as he. "All you care about is your damned drug and your stinking research!" A look of pain flashed quickly across his features, but she convinced herself she had imagined it. "It can't be love, Captain," she said scornfully. "And you can't even come up with anything flattering, like—"

"Ah, yes! Mad desire. But then, I've told you that mad desire is my main aim. I've tasted the forbidden, golden fruit, my love, and can't quite forget it. My fault, of course. But I really take such things to heart, Mrs. Denver. You were living like a vestal virgin, and my stinking research brought a halt to it all—so totally, it seems, that I changed you completely. Now you're ready for anything in pants!"

"Oh!" She couldn't move, so she made a wild attempt to bite him, but he crawled over her, securing her wrists with one of his own, barely allowing her to keep her head out of water.

"You're ever so concerned about your reputation. The little coral princess, sworn to celibacy to honor a dead man. But it would be far more honorable to marry one man than to run around with a score of them, wouldn't it?"

"Let go of me! I swear, I will have you court-martialed!"

"Yes, you keep making that promise," he said impassively. "I think you should accept my solution to your problems."

"I haven't got any problems! Or at least I won't once you're off my island!"

He just shook his head, sighing. His one hand was free beneath the water, and he used it, stroking her ribs which were bare and susceptible to his touch and the lull of the water.

Then his fingers were feathering lower, rimming the band of her bikini, far too low on her hips.

"Stop it!" she raged.

His fingers went lower, around to the base of her spine, then back again. The bikini slipped against the force of his hand. He had such easy access. . . .

Then his fingers were between her thighs, touching her so that she gasped, shooting her through with liquid heat. He smiled, having found the warmth and proof of arousal that he desired. And he used that proof, moving his touch in a subtle rhythm.

"Quit it, Mike!" she gasped in a plea.

It got her nowhere, not really. Her bikini shifted back into position, but his arms were suddenly around her; his face, strained and intense, was over hers.

"Why? Why do you keep lying to me?" he demanded in a thunderous, frustrated voice. "And, by God, worse still, why do you keep lying to yourself?"

He didn't expect an answer; she couldn't have given him one. His mouth covered hers, searching, tender. His arms were so gentle around her, his kiss so cajoling, so caressing, his tongue a stroke of love and power that filled her. . . .

"Katrina! Katrina! Oh!"

She knew the voice. It came out of a fog. Then it struck her with crystal clarity. It was Nancy's voice. Nancy Denver's voice.

"Oh, no!"

She tore away from Michael; this time he instantly let her go. He was already on his feet, ready to help her to hers.

But she ignored his outstretched hand. She was staring with horror at the beach. Frank's motorboat was pulled up there, and he and Jason were busy securing it high on the sand.

Nancy was in cutoffs and a shirt; they had obviously gone to the mainland to pick her up and take her fishing with them. And she had obviously seen the bodies in the sand, and worried.

And now, across the thirty yards between the sand and the mangroves, she was smiling at Katrina very ruefully.

"See you at the house!" she called gaily, and turned away.

"Come on," Mike began.

Katrina slapped his hand away with a vengeance. "I want to die!" she shouted at him. "I'm not drunk and I don't have a hangover and I want to die anyway!"

"Katrina."

She staggered to her feet and burst into tears. For James. For her mother-in-law. For herself. And for the man she just couldn't allow herself to have.

"No! Leave me alone! I beg you, leave me alone!"

He stared at her for a long moment, hands on his hips, silver eyes cold.

"The offer still stands, Katrina."

"What offer?" she choked out.

"Marriage—if you ever come up with the courage to accept it."

He strode past her, heedless that he had left his mask and flippers in the waves. Katrina sank back down into the water.

He was gone, and she just sat there, silently crying, listening to the surf, to the breeze, and feeling numb.

She had to go back to her house. She had to face Nancy. That much she knew.

Wearily she stood, and started back.

CHAPTER ELEVEN

Everything seemed so normal!

Nancy smiled at her when she walked in. "I don't mean to be interfering, dear, but we've got lunch under control if you'd like to step into the shower."

"Lovely. Thanks." She hesitated. "I'm glad you could make it out today, Mom. Jason has missed you."

Nancy chuckled, slicing a tomato. "I'm not so sure he has; I can't quite compare with the excitement of the Navy." Then she turned around and Katrina saw that things weren't quite as normal as they looked. "I—I hope it's all right that I came."

"You're always welcome here!" Katrina said fiercely.

"Thank you, dear." She was staring down at her tomatoes. It looked as if her eyes might be brimming with tears.

I'm so sorry! Katrina wanted to cry out. *So very, very sorry!*

But she couldn't apologize out loud, and she really wasn't certain exactly what it was that she'd be apologizing for. Except that surely, surely, she had hurt this lovely woman she had considered a second mother all her life.

She walked up behind her and slipped her arms around her waist, resting her head against her shoulder. "I love you."

Nancy paused, squeezing the slim hands about her waist, reaching back to pat Katrina's cheek.

"I love you too. You know that."

Katrina nodded, then suddenly became aware that both

Jason and Frank were curiously silent. She moved away from Nancy, smiled faintly, and raced for the shower.

Lunch was nice, except that Frank offered her a beer and the smell of it almost nauseated her again. He saw her face and laughed. "I forgot your hangover! Cruel of me!"

Nancy looked up at her, a smile playing about her lips. "You do look a bit ashen."

Katrina wanted to kick Frank. He was watching her diabolically, as if he knew he was making a point that she didn't want him to make at all.

Katrina bit into her sandwich. "I feel fine."

A slight frown touched Nancy's brow. "You did make it home all right? I asked Frank to go with you, but he was adamant that you would be all right."

"I—I made it home fine."

"What's everybody talking about?" Jason demanded.

"Nothing—" Katrina began.

"Your mom had two white knights fighting over her last night, Jase. Just like the fairy tale princess!"

"Frank!" This time Katrina did kick him.

"Ouch! Oh, she's beautiful, but vicious!" he groaned.

"Frank, I'm going to get a lot more vicious if you don't shut up!" Katrina wailed.

"What happened? What happened?" Jason pleaded.

"Yes, what did happen?" Nancy queried more softly.

But then Frank, at long last, decided to extricate her from the mess he had caused. "Not too much, really. Katrina just got in the middle of something that has been going on a long time, it seems. Anyway, the best man won. She just went to dinner with the wrong one."

"Who won? Mike won?" Jason's eyes gleamed with pleasure.

"Yep," Frank assured him.

"Wow!" He looked at his mother. "Mike brought you home?"

"Yes," Katrina mumbled warily, staring intently down at her food.

Nancy was looking at her with interest. "That's the captain I met last night? The young man you were with this morning?"

"You were with him this morning?" Jason cried out.

"I was—I was out on the reefs this morning. He just managed to stumble along, I guess," Katrina murmured. She sipped her tea. It didn't help. They were all staring at her. She felt like the main attraction at a circus, and she wished to God she knew what Nancy was really thinking.

But Nancy wasn't going to say any more. She picked up her sandwich. "Oh, Frank, Katrina. Don't let me forget; I have a number for you to call. Some old friends of Dad's want to make a reservation for night fishing. Probably toward the end of next week. Do you think you're free? They're down for a convention from Ohio, and he'd really like them to enjoy the water."

"We'll make sure that they do," Frank promised.

"Of course," Katrina agreed. And then Nancy was asking Jason about school and how he was doing with his homework.

She was off the hook; she could breathe a little more easily.

For the moment, at least.

Entering his lab, Mike was so tense and distracted that he swore softly and perched on his stool, without noticing the tall, very pretty blonde standing by the cages, watching him.

It was several seconds before he became aware that someone was there.

But then his features lit with a beautiful smile, and the hard glitter of his eyes softened.

"Toni!"

She laughed delightedly, running into his arms. He hugged her fiercely, then set her free, looking anxiously into her features, as always the father, assuring himself that she was well, and in one piece.

"I didn't know you were coming today!"

"I finished up at the university early," she told him, then

frowned. "I talked to Stan, and he seemed to be concerned about you."

"Was he?" A small pulse of annoyance beat against Mike's temple. "I'm fine. What has he been telling you?"

Toni searched her father's face. "Only that there's been a few problems with the project," she lied smoothly. She shrugged, still watching him. "Anyway, I was just anxious to see you."

"Honey"—he hugged her again—"I'm always anxious to see you! So tell me, what did you decide? How did you like the school?"

Toni told him about the professors she had met, and that she thought she had found a roommate. "An Army brat—just like I'm a Navy brat!" Toni laughed. "And it's really super, because we can compare all the places we've lived."

"Well, good," he murmured, and threaded his fingers through his still damp hair. He stared at her with a paternal eye. "They do call it 'Sunshine U,' you know."

"Oh, Dad! The medical school is great."

"You're not in medical school yet."

"But I will be," Toni said confidently. "And there are some programs I'm sure I can horn my way into ahead of time. Dad, you said that I could go to college wherever I wanted."

He nodded slowly. Wherever she went, Toni would do okay. She was so responsible, so mature.

She had grown into such a beauty, he mused, staring at her tenderly. A good five feet eight inches, a golden blonde, just as her mother had been. For a moment he felt a little bit awed that she was actually his, this lovely young woman. And then he closed his eyes, very grateful that she was. They'd shared the loss of her mother; they'd battled through her teen years. But they'd stayed fiercely close, and she had been, through the years, his greatest supporter.

He caught her hand. "Okay, Sunshine U it is! But for now, you came to work, so get cracking."

Toni laughed, indicating his bathing trunks. "Looks like you've been working—real hard!" she teased.

"Mmm," he murmured. "But then I'm the boss, remember? I want some soil samples from the pool, and I want you to pull more vegetation for me too. Good hired help is hard to find these days, I swear!" He moaned, then smiled at her. "But if we get done early, I'll take you out for dinner."

"And drinks?"

He shrugged. "Are you of legal age in this state?"

"No."

"There's your answer."

"Oh, Dad!" she sighed. "Okay, I'll settle for ice cream."

It was on Monday night that Katrina first saw the blonde. She had ambled out to the beach, tried to convince herself that she wasn't trying to run into Mike. She gave up when she saw that the lab was dark, and started back through the trail.

But the sound of a motor and that of voices held her still on the trail, and to her horror, she remained there, hiding and watching.

It was Mike. And he wasn't alone. He was with the blonde.

Katrina couldn't see her clearly. She did see that she was tall, slim, and sleek, with a shoulder-length cascade of golden curls.

And Katrina saw Michael's arm around her, with the greatest affection. They were chatting about food, laughing together.

And they disappeared into the lab together.

Her face flaming, Katrina raced back to her house. Thank God that Jason was sleeping! She was free to run straight into her room, throw herself onto the bed, and indulge in a storm of tears. Damn him! First a brunette—then a blonde! What he apparently wanted was a harem, not a wife.

But of course, he had never been serious about his offer of marriage. And of course, she would never take it. It would hurt her, it would be unfair to James, it would devastate Nancy and Ted.

Or would it? Katrina swung her legs over the side of the bed and pressed her forehead tightly between her palms.

No . . . Nancy would understand. Ted would understand. Katrina forced herself to admit that she had been hiding behind them as much as she'd been hiding behind her own walls.

"Because I am a coward," she whispered aloud.

But wasn't she right to be one? Wasn't Michael Taylor proving that most men were incapable of the real caring she had known?

"Cheats! They are all cheats!" she whispered aloud. She should call his bluff. She should go running down to the lab and interrupt whatever he was doing with the blonde and tell him that she'd decided to take him up on his offer!

But she wouldn't do it. She knew she wouldn't.

In the morning she felt so horrible that she took Jason to school, came home, went back to bed, and, exhausted, slept again.

Mike was studying a blood sample from a squirrel when the phone rang. He ignored it, knowing that Toni would pick it up.

"Dad, it's Stan."

"Ask him if I can call him back."

"He says it's important."

Mike sighed, stretched, then accepted the cordless phone from his daughter's hand.

"Yeah, Stan."

"I need to see you. About that phone call Katrina got. You know, telling her that the project was canceled."

"All right, I'll be right over to the ship," Mike muttered.

"No!" Stan protested with a laugh. "The admiral is still ready to bite your head off. He says you go on leave, take out his best nurse, then leave her stranded with a fellow officer you've beaten up! You're not his favorite person at the moment. Meet me on Islamorada."

"Where?"

Stan hesitated a moment, then chuckled. "At the scene of

the crime, I guess. I might as well get to eat at this Lucky Lobster too. And by the way, you're buying."

He broke the connection. Mike frowned and handed the phone back to Toni.

"What's up?" she asked him.

"I'm not sure. I've got to run over to Islamorada." He paused, then grinned. "Okay, you've got the afternoon off."

"Good, I'll go sun on the beach."

"No, there're still sailors all over the place," he said darkly, causing Toni to laugh.

"Real wolves, huh, Dad. Hoowwl!"

"Howl, yourself!" he retorted, then hesitated as he doffed his lab coat. "Go lie by the pool, huh? It's a little better protected."

"Can I go topless there?"

"No!"

"Only teasing!" Toni promised. She blew him a little kiss as he left, and he cást her a warning eye.

"Well?" Mike asked Stan, nursing a beer. They sat at the same table he had shared with Amy.

Stan took a deep breath. "All right. I managed to track down the two Marines who were on the island before you came in that morning. They couldn't find her—apparently she was at the pool. So they said to headquarters."

"And?"

"Well, they were on radio. And that storm must have already been brewing up. They got a lot of static."

"And no answer?"

"No, they got an answer."

"Well?"

"They were told that Katrina Denver was definitely off the island. That they were free to give you the go-ahead to go on in. Neither of them would swear to it, but they think that it was Captain Stradford on the radio."

"Al!"

"But I can't prove any of it, Mike."

Mike shook his head, amazed that Stradford would go to such lengths to discredit him.

"What are you going to do?"

He shook his head. "I don't know."

"Well, you can't go beat him up," Stan said philosophically. "You've already done that."

Mike flashed him a sizzling stare.

"Well?"

Mike laughed suddenly. "I don't know. I honestly don't know." He lifted his beer to Stan. "Cheers."

Frank Denver thought that he had been hallucinating when he first walked past the pool. He stopped his anxious strides for the house, spun around, and discovered that he hadn't imagined the blonde at all.

God, she was beautiful! Long, leggy, and with a fan of hair so golden beneath the sun it might have been cast from its flame.

She was just there, stretched out on a towel in a snow-white one-piece bathing suit, reading an anatomy book, of all damn things. Frank forgot his concern about Katrina. He forgot everything.

He just stared at the blonde.

And at last she looked up.

"Hi."

"Hi." She looked familiar. No, she couldn't be. He'd have remembered her if he had ever met her before.

"Are you a sailor?" she asked him.

"No, I'm a—uh—businessman, I guess. Well, yes, I sail, but not with the Navy. Are you with the Navy?"

She smiled. "Sort of. I'm with Mike Taylor." She stood up, smiling, stretching out a hand. "I'm Antoinette Taylor."

Taylor! Oh, hell! For a minute Frank froze. His lips curled into a sneer of contempt. Here he'd practically thrown his sister-in-law at him, and he had this sweet young thing as a wife!

"You're—his—wife?" Frank stuttered out.

She started to laugh, her eyes as light as summer clouds.

"Does that mean that he looks young—or that I look old? I'm his daughter, not his wife."

"Oh," Frank said, relieved. Except that . . . to have a daughter, you had to have had a wife somewhere along the line.

He sat and stared at the long, glorious length of her, and reminded himself strictly that she had to be a very young thing.

"Is—uh—your mother here?" he asked her.

"My mother's been dead over ten years," she replied huskily, then demanded, "Okay—who are you?"

"Frank Denver," Frank replied a little absently.

"Denver! Then you're related to—Katrina. I'd love to meet her."

"Katrina?"

"Please? Would you introduce me?"

He hesitated a little warily, then smiled.

"Sounds good to me. Come on."

Frank led Toni through the trail to the house. His anxiety for Katrina returned as he pounded on the door and received no answer. But just when he was about to panic and break through it, the door opened.

Katrina was standing there, sleepy eyed, in a robe, her hair a flame of wild beauty around her delicate features.

"Oh, Frank," she murmured, stepping back for him to come in. "Sorry, I was sleep—"

She broke off abruptly, staring at the tall blonde, who was looking very, very svelt and shapely in a white bathing suit.

Oh, hell! Katrina thought instantly. *This is just what I need! His other women in my house!*

And she was young. Really young. *Cradle robber!* Katrina accused Mike inwardly, and with a wrench of her heart.

"You're so tiny!" the blonde suddenly gasped.

Katrina took a deep breath and tried to tell herself that this woman was barely more than a child.

"Sorry. It's the way I came. Frank—"

Frank was wearing a devil's smile on his face, and Katrina

was suddenly furious, certain that he'd brought the blonde to her doorstep just to torture her.

"Katrina," he interrupted her. "I'd like you to meet Antoinette Taylor."

The floor seemed to slip out from beneath her; she thought she was going to fall. So Mike was a liar on top of everything else! Running around making marriage proposals when he'd already robbed the cradle for a bride!

And she probably would have fallen, except that Frank caught her arm. Then Antoinette Taylor started to speak.

"I'd like to speak with you about my father, Mrs. Denver."

"Your father?" She barely managed to whisper the words.

"Yes, my father."

Katrina didn't know whether to laugh or cry at her own foolishness. But she hadn't known . . .

She hadn't known anything about him, really. She'd never bothered to ask. She'd always been so wrapped up in herself.

The realization was sickening. How could she have been so callous?

"Ah, please, come in, Antoinette," she murmured.

"Toni," the girl said, but she didn't seem all that terribly friendly.

"I'll put some coffee on," Frank murmured.

Katrina nodded absently. She sat on the sofa. Toni Taylor sat down beside her.

"I'll be blunt, Mrs. Denver. I don't want you to sue my father. I don't want you to ruin his life, or his career, or his dreams."

"I'm not—"

"Maybe you don't fully understand things, Mrs. Denver, and maybe you should. I understand that you're a widow, and I'm very, very sorry. But you're not the only person alive to ever know hurt. My father had been wounded in Saigon, and my mother went to bring him home. Except that some kids made a raid on her hotel, throwing grenades everywhere. Fifteen people died in agony—including my mother. But my father didn't go crazy. He tried to pick up the pieces, and started up his work on 44DFS."

Katrina couldn't seem to hear; it was as if the ocean were rushing over her, again and again.

Frank was suddenly standing in front of her.

"I'm running back to Islamorada for Jason," he said very softly. "It's time. Do you hear me?"

"Yes."

"The coffee is done."

"Thanks, Frank," she managed to whisper.

The door closed behind him. Toni was still sitting on the couch.

Katrina burst into tears.

"Mrs. Denver, Mrs. Denver . . ."

"Toni, I'm so sorry! So very, very sorry!"

"Oh, Lord!" Toni groaned. "I didn't mean . . . I just wanted you to see, oh, nooo. . . ."

She put her arms around Katrina and hugged her awkwardly. "I thought you were out to get him, and I . . . please, stop crying. It was a long time ago now. I—"

Katrina at last managed to draw her hands from her face, to wipe her tears away.

She never knew exactly what Toni saw in her eyes, but the girl suddenly stopped speaking and just stared at her.

Then she gasped. "You're in love with him, aren't you!"

"I—I don't know."

She realized that she was making a blithering idiot of herself.

In front of his daughter.

Katrina tried to straighten, tried to dignify herself. "But, Toni, I knew that I wasn't going to sue him. And he knew it too."

"Oh." It was Toni's turn to be perplexed.

Katrina snuffled against her will, then smiled ruefully. "You really didn't make me do that. It was just me—oh, never mind. Would you like some coffee? It's one thing that Frank is very good at."

"I—uh—yes, please!"

Katrina fixed coffee; they brought it back to the sofa. And then Katrina found herself asking about Mike, and Toni was answering her, talking about the different places they'd been, telling her about their home outside of Washington.

Then Toni asked awkwardly, "Is my father in love with you?"

"I—uh—don't know."

"You could find out," Toni suggested.

"Oh." A wistful smile played across Katrina's mouth. "How?"

"Ask him, of course," Toni said.

And then the door opened; Frank was back with Jason.

"Hi—you must be Toni!" Jason said cheerfully. "I was wondering when you'd get here."

"Jason," Katrina said, accepting the absent little hug he gave her as he smiled up at Toni. "You knew that Toni was coming here?"

"Of course. Mike told me." He smiled at Toni. "He talks about you all the time."

"Does he?" Toni laughed. "All good, I hope."

"He says you're the best."

Frank was watching Katrina from across the room. She smiled at him, then stood up suddenly. "Would you all excuse me for a few minutes? I'm going to run in and get dressed, then I think I'll take a walk down to the lab."

"I'll go with you," Jason began.

Frank caught his shoulders. "Not this time, sport. I'll bet if you wait here with Toni and me, your Mom will bring Mike back for dinner. You have to help Toni and me get the dinner going, okay?"

"He had to run into Islamorada, Mrs. Denver. But if he isn't back now, he will be soon," Toni offered.

Katrina nodded and smiled as she hurried toward her bedroom to change. She would wait just as long as it took.

CHAPTER TWELVE

Michael paused in the doorway of the lab; the light that filtered in from the outside was muted and shadowed by the palms that waved overhead. Dusk was coming, blurring his vision.

But he could make out the figure of a woman, perched on his stool, her long legs bare beneath a knee-length skirt of flowy material, sandaled feet twined around the stool.

It wasn't Toni. She was way too small to be Toni.

"Hi."

Her voice was husky. He closed the door behind him and felt the pulse of his heart take flight. It was a halter dress she was wearing, light and cool, with blue and white stripes. Her hair was curling over her shoulders in rich waves, catching the muted sunlight from beyond, gleaming like dark fire.

"Hi," he said warily.

She left the stool. Gracefully and slowly, like a cat, as fluid as sun rippling against water, she came to him, stood on tiptoe, cupped his face between her hands . . .

And kissed him. Lips pressed lightly to his, her dainty tongue slipping out to rub and flick against his mouth, growing bolder, sliding against his teeth, filling his mouth. Her fingers were in his hair, her breasts crushed to his chest, her small form searing against his.

He kissed her back. It was the only natural thing to do.

His arms swept around her, bringing her closer. His mouth was very hungry for all that she offered. His hands were touching her, lifting her higher against him, closer, close enough to feel his heartbeat, the ragged tear of his breath, the strength of his need for her.

It was such a precious moment. The feel of her fingers against his cheek, the soft moan that echoed in her throat, the soft and wonderful shape of her, in his arms, promising paradise.

But then something in him grew cold and wary. He held her away from him and stared at her. But her head was bent, and he could not see her eyes.

Instinctively, he looked around the lab. The desk was locked, the drawers were locked. Nothing was amiss. But he was afraid of a promise that might not be true, and he spoke to her harshly.

"What have you been into?"

She raised her head to his. Even in the shadow her eyes were brilliant with a thousand facets of color, greens and blues, and shades in between.

"Nothing, Captain. Not a damn thing."

"Then why are you here?" he asked her hoarsely, and he was on the stool then, ridiculously afraid to trust himself to stand.

She started walking to him again, that cat walk, sleek and sultry and eliciting desire within him.

"I've decided to accept your proposal," she said lightly. And then she reached for him again. Her fingers went to the tie at his neck, quickly, deftly, undoing it, then more slowly, with infinite finesse, pulling it from around his neck, and dropping it to the floor.

He caught her fingers and forced her to look at him. "I'm not in the mood for games, Mrs. Denver. Start something now, and you'd damn well better finish it."

"But I intend to finish it, Captain!" she told him, eyes wide and sincere. She tugged her hand gently from his grip; her fingers moved to his shirt.

"Don't play with me."

"I'm not. I'm going to marry you."

"Why?"

He caught both her hands and found that he was standing

again, forcing her back this time, back, until she reached the wall. And then he placed his hands—still locked with hers—on either side of her head, pinning her there.

And she smiled, lashes lowering slightly, completely unaware of the blazing complexities of his ragged emotions. Or maybe very aware of them. . . .

"Why?" he repeated hoarsely.

And her eyes were on his again, pure like the sky, a mystery like the sea.

"Well," she said softly, "I'm not marrying you to keep from getting into trouble." She grinned a bit mockingly. "Not for stud service."

"Go on."

"And I'm not marrying you because it might keep me from testifying against you in court. We'll never go to court."

"Katrina—"

"I am marrying you because I don't think that I could bear it if you left my life."

He closed his eyes. "Go on!" he urged her tensely.

"Because I want you so badly that I had to come to you. I dream of you during the nights. I remember the way that you held me. I remember, in fact, each and everything you did to me, and each and everything I did to you. Because . . ."

"Because?" he thundered.

"Because . . ." she whispered very softly, "I think I love you."

"You think?"

"A kiss could convince me."

There was the slightest hesitance, the slightest fear in her voice, and it touched every raw cord within him.

"Oh, God!" he breathed, and he caught her chin very tenderly in his hand, stroking her cheek with his thumb. Then he lowered his head to hers, sweetly, sweetly savoring the taste of her lips, the fullness of her mouth, the feel of her body against his, her perfumed scent, as light and as heady as a breeze. Her arms slipped around him, and she clung to him, pressed against him as if she wanted to become a part of him. The softest sound, like a little sob, tore from her; her fingers coursed over his shoulders and back, elegant, powerful, the ripple of her nails causing him to groan, to tear away at last.

"Well?" she demanded breathlessly, and there was a sparkle of tears in her eyes.

"Well?"

And she choked back a laugh—or a sob. "There it is, Captain Taylor. On the floor for you. Bleeding and bare! My heart! Haven't you anything to say?"

He grinned ruefully, nodded, pressed her back against his length, cherishing her as he held her.

"I love you, Katrina."

"Again," she whispered.

And he complied, saying the words over and over as he kissed her bare shoulders, her throat, her lips.

"Where do you sleep, Captain?" she asked him.

"In a bed, in back."

"Lead me to it."

"Gladly!"

He had her hand; he had started eagerly striding toward a door in the back when he stopped abruptly, pulling her back into his arms.

"We can't."

"Yes, we can. I know exactly how. Problems, suddenly, Captain?"

He rewarded her taunt with a stinging blow on the rump.

"Ouch! What—"

"You'll have problems soon, Mrs. Denver, if you don't learn some respect! Just for that, I'll see that you spend a day incapable of walking." Then he sobered. "Katrina, my daughter is here. She'll probably be back any minute."

Katrina's eyes narrowed lazily. "No, she won't."

"How—"

"Toni is baby-sitting."

"How—"

"Oh, please shut up and let me explain later! We're supposed to be back for dinner, so I'd say an hour is all that we have."

He stared down at her, a little incredulous, a little doubtful. The answering flame in her eyes assured him, the touch of her fingers along his arms decided him.

"You're right," he murmured, tugging at the halter tie around her neck. "I've an hour to make sure you can barely move—doubting my prowess!"

Her dress fell to the floor. She stepped outside of it, then kicked it and her sandals away. Clad in the flimsiest excuse for panties he'd ever seen, she took a step toward him and started on his buttons once again. He slipped his fingers beneath the panty rim, stroking her rounded buttocks.

"Stop!" she whispered. "I'll never get these buttons!"

"Oh, the hell with them!" Mike laughed, ripping his shirt open. She laughed; her fingers fell to his belt buckle and he lost patience completely, sweeping her into his arms.

He locked the door to the lab, swung around, and carried her to the bunk in the back, hobbling in his efforts to remove his shoes. Katrina awaited him on the bunk, stretching luxuriously, wondering why and how she had ever denied herself this happiness. It didn't matter, she was with him now.

He was finally naked, but she could wait no longer. She sprang to her knees and enwrapped his torso, relishing the tremor and constriction of muscle. Her kisses fell over his chest, darting whispers of heat and moisture. She clutched him, and loved him, coming alive at his hoarse whispers, deviously determined to make him half crazy, determined to give herself the ultimate pleasure of driving him mad. She wanted to love him, love the wonderful, potent force of his desire.

"Katrina . . ." He breathed her name as the splendor of her kiss racked through his body. And he clutched her shoulders, drawing her up, hard against his chest, and then beneath him. His hands cupped her breast, her breast filled his mouth. She moved deliciously beneath him, and in a frenzy his hands molded her body, his mouth tasted all of it.

In moments she was whimpering, a wildcat, twisting, arching, a fury of sensuality, longing to be a part of him.

"Hmmm," he groaned delightedly, holding her still to watch her face as he moved over her.

"Are you sure you weren't into the drug cabinets?"

She heatedly clasped his neck, bringing his lips to hers. "You are the drug, my love. Your hands, your touch, your eyes, your—"

"My what?"

"Come here, I'll whisper. Oh!"

He was inside her, shuddering, remembering. Loving her now more than he ever could have before. Whispering her name. Relishing the sound of his own on her lips.

Knowing that love was real, and that it was theirs.

Mike rose first; Katrina tried to snuggle beneath the covers.

"Up!" he told her, tapping her bottom.

"Stop!" she moaned.

"We have to get back to the dinner. To the children, remember, Mrs. Denver?"

She tried to rise and failed. His arms came around her to support her, and she cast him a baleful glance.

"When you take revenge, you take revenge!"

"Complaining?"

"No!" she laughed. "No, never."

"I can always carry you. Thank God you're so light."

"Don't be ridiculous! What would the children think?" She groaned. "Oh! And Frank is there too! He's going to taunt me to death!"

Mike shook his head. "He's a great guy," he said a little huskily. "Very special." He caught Katrina's hand suddenly. "Katrina, you don't have to lose them, you know. You're marrying me—not giving up anything, none of the love that came with a past life."

She touched his cheek, warmed by the care in his eyes. "I know. Maybe it just took me a while to understand it."

He smiled and released her. Back in the lab he picked up her dress and threw it at her.

"Come on! I have to make the announcement before you chicken out on me."

Katrina stumbled into her dress. "I won't chicken out!"

He cocked his head to the side and grinned at her. "Keep 'em hungry!" he teased. "Works every time."

"Oh, do shut up! And let's go!"

Dinner was nice. Jason was ecstatic. Toni was a little stunned, but she handled it all well.

And Frank didn't tease her at all. He broke out a bottle of wine, and wore a self-satisfied smirk all night as if he had planned the entire thing himself.

The next afternoon Mike took Katrina over to an out-of-the-way place in Largo.

Katrina wanted at least a month to plan for a wedding. "It really is so sudden! And—"

"And what?"

"I can't help it. I'm very traditional. I want organ music, flowers, and wonderfully solemn vows, blessed by God. I want the Denvers there—Frank and Ted and Nancy, and—oh, Mike! I hope they really understand. They mean so much to me. It wasn't just James, you see. I grew up spending half my time in their house. Either I was there, or James was at my house. Oh! And speaking of my mother"—Katrina suddenly laughed—"she's going to want to take charge. I'm not going to let her, of course."

"Your poor mother!" he sympathised, but then he shook his head. "Such a whirl of energy—and she gave you such a lovely temper!"

"I haven't got a bad temper."

"I have endured a few slaps that say differently."

"You deserved a lot more than slapped cheeks!"

After a long lunch they strolled along the dock. Rock Cay was a small dot in the southern distance.

"It's going to be hard to leave." Katrina sighed, leaning against him.

He frowned, resting his chin on the top of her head. "Where are we going?"

"I don't know. Where *are* we going?"

"Wherever you get sent next," Katrina murmured, and he whirled her around to face him.

"You mean you were ready to pick up and go—anywhere?"

Katrina blushed, staring out at the horizon. "Well, of course, you're in the Navy."

She was startled when he swung her back around, hugging her fiercely. "Kat . . . I can't tell you how damn good it feels to hear that. But we're not going anywhere."

"We're not?"

"Oh, on a honeymoon, yeah. But we're going to stay on Rock Cay. I'm retiring."

"Mike!" she gasped. "No! That's your life, your career! I can't ask you to—to give it up."

"I don't intend to give up what I do, any more than I expect you to stay out of the reefs. I thought I'd start up a small private practice. On Largo, or Islamorada. Just for a few days a week. Because I never intend to quit with the 44DFS project. And I've a few other—"

"Bless us and save us!" Katrina prayed vehemently. "Go on."

"Go on? That's it. We'll just leave the lab where it is. What do you think?"

She chuckled. "I don't know what I think about the lab, but, oh, Mike! If you're serious, I'm thrilled."

"I am serious. Jason won't have to change schools, and Toni will be in Miami. It's perfect. And you won't have to leave Frank and your business." He hesitated just a second, stroking the length of her hair. "Katrina, I went to see Nancy Denver this morning."

"You—did?"

"I told her that I wanted her to know that I loved you very much, and that I love her grandson too. And that I hoped that I wouldn't change anything, that she'd be every bit as welcome on Rock Cay as she has always been."

"Oh, Mike! What did she say?"

"That she loves you too. That she hopes we'll be very happy."

"Oh, Mike." Tears stung her eyes, tears of happiness and pain. "It was his island, really. James's. His dream. His Eden. And it killed him."

Mike wrapped his arms around her tightly. "The island didn't kill him, Katrina. Life is something which we have to live with faith. You have to really believe sometimes. Damn, Katrina, I was the one in the service! Yet Margo was the one who was killed. There's no justice to it. I stayed sane by believing that there was a greater world beyond ours, that she was beyond all pain. And by believing that I could make a change in this one."

Katrina turned and hugged him very tightly. "You're a dreamer!" she accused him softly. "But you do make it a better world!"

"If I can have you in it, then that's all I really want."

Stan had let Mike know that Al Stradford was going in to Islamorada to the bar.

Mike followed him over.

He waited until he was seated alone at a booth, idly sipping at a whiskey. Then he slipped across from him.

Al glared at him warily. "What are you after, Taylor? You managed to get things your way—so what more do you want?"

"Actually, I want to thank you. Then warn you."

"You are crazier than a Cheshire cat!" Al accused him. He watched him for a moment, certain that Mike meant to lash out at him any second.

"Settle down, Stradford," Mike said, smiling. "If I'd wanted another brawl, I'd have said so."

Al watched him for several seconds, then decided that he was telling the truth. "Want a drink?"

"Yeah. I'll take a beer."

Al kept watching him as they signaled for the waitress.

"What is it?" Al suddenly exploded. "Come on, Taylor, you've already proven you could beat me."

Mike laughed. "Is that it, Al? Hey, life is always like the rungs of a ladder. So I can beat you. Maybe the next guy will be able to beat me."

"Oh, yeah?" Al arched a brow as he lifted his glass to Mike. "Not you, Taylor. You're always the damn hero. And nobody likes a damn hero time after time."

Mike made an impatient gesture. "I'm not a hero, Al."

"No? You pulled me out of a sinking ship."

"Damn it, anyone would have done that, Al!" He shook his head. "Is that it? You've spent all these years working behind my back to sabatoge projects because I pulled you out of a ship? Hell—maybe I should have let you drown!"

Al hesitated, then shrugged, apparently having decided it didn't matter much anymore what he said. "All right, maybe that started it. But if I came to the admiral with one idea, damned if you didn't give him another one. A better one. If I saw a woman I liked, she was already sleeping with you. When bombs were exploding around us, you just kept working without missing a stroke, and I thought I'd die of fright every damn time. Every damn place I wanted to be, Taylor, you'd reached it already. Everything I wanted to be —you already were."

Mike shook his head. "Al, you ass! I've been so scared I was afraid I'd run away with someone's wound half sewn up. And I've been on the admiral's black list, and I've been turned down half a dozen times on what I thought were brilliant ideas."

Al hadn't seemed to have heard. "Even the girl the other night. What was it with you, Taylor? She was out with me— so you just had to have her instead."

Mike shook his head, then drained the beer the waitress had brought him. "That's what I came to thank you for. I'm marrying her, Al."

That caught Stradford's attention.

"You—you're getting married again?"

"Yeah. And it's thanks to the fact that you arranged to see that she wound up stuck on the island with 44DFS."

"That's a crock! You can't prove it! But he had been caught off guard, and his voice lacked conviction.

"No, I can't prove it. But I know it. You called and told her we'd canceled, and you told the Marines she was gone."

"I—yeah, I did it," Al rasped out wearily. "You can't prove it, though. What—what are you going to do?"

"I'm going to retire."

It seemed that Al held his breath for a long, long time.

"And you're going to let me off? Just like that."

Mike stood, grimacing down at him. "Maybe. We'll see. I expect you to do something yourself, Stradford. Let your conscience be your guide."

Mike left him, squaring his shoulders, his smile just a little bit bitter.

Katrina was there when he returned to the island, waiting for him on the beach. The wind rippled her hair; her feet were bare. He beached the launch, then came to her, wrapping his arms around her, feeling long silken tendrils of her hair blow and weave about him like a delicate web.

She kissed him lightly, slipped an arm around his waist, and started for the trail.

He pulled her back. "Wait a minute, Katrina. I have to tell you something."

She paused, smiling a little hesitantly at his tone.

"What?"

He placed his hands on her shoulders. "Katrina, I found out who called you about the project. It was Al Stradford. He wanted the project blown."

Katrina stared at him searchingly. "Can you prove it?"

"No."

"But?"

"I just talked to him."

Again, her beautiful sea eyes searched his. "And?"

"It's difficult; he's a good doctor, and a good scientist. I'm hoping that he'll turn himself in, and that the Navy will go easy on him.

She touched his hair. "Let's wait and see, shall we?"

He nodded.

A secret smile was on her lips as she took his arm again and they walked back to the house.

Jason and Harry were playing a game of backgammon in the living room. They could hear Toni humming in the kitchen.

Mike had barely closed the door when the phone started ringing. Toni answered it, then came around the kitchen door.

"Oh, Dad! You are back."

"Was it for me?"

"Yes, and it was rather peculiar. It was Captain Stradford. He said he wanted to volunteer his services for the 44DFS project. For whatever you may need."

Katrina and Mike stared at each other, then grinned.

Jason shook his head and stared up at Toni.

"Grown-ups are strange!" he concluded.

Katrina dragged Mike with her and plopped down beside Jason, hugging him so he squirmed.

"Hey! You're the one who wanted a mad scientist for a stepdad, huh?"

And Jason had to smile. "Yeah, I guess that I did!"

Epilogue

"Mom! Mom! Come quick!"

Katrina started slightly. Usually, she would have been attuned to the urgency in Jason's voice and responded instantly to his call. Somewhere in her subconscious, though, she knew that it was a cry of laughter and excitement, not of fear. And today . . .

Something about today had cast her so deeply into her own thoughts that she remained where she was, cocooned in a dream world.

It might have been the wind; it might have been the lulling dip of the palm fronds, or the slow ripples moving across the surface of the pond. There was a scent of wild orchids in the air today too.

She was remembering their wedding. Her parents had been there, as well as Jason, Toni, Frank, the Denvers, Harry, and what seemed like half of the Second Fleet. A score of Navy men and a few scattered Marines all had come to give their best. The admiral had been there, as had Stan, smiling away as if he had planned the entire thing himself.

There had been a honeymoon, in Switzerland. They were accustomed to sun and sand and the beach, so snowcapped mountains and cozy fires were a romantic change.

But still . . .

For Katrina the best time had been here. Here by the pool, with the sun beating down on them, with Mike swearing that he had fallen in love the second he had seen her, a wild thing, bursting from the shade of the palms and the tangle of the subtropical jungle like a goddess set to do battle. . . .

"Mom!"

This time Jason's shriek did penetrate the fog of her thoughts. She catapulted to her feet, spinning like a dancer on her bare toes for a moment as she tried to locate his position.

South . . . she was certain that the cry had come from the south, by the second inland pool.

She ran, led by instinct. Past a patch of crotons, wild hibiscus, and bitter cherry. She found the path, which was shaded by a line of palm trees. It was almost dusk, and the sun was casting patterns of red and orange and primitive pink.

"Jason!"

He was there, and Harry was there.

Jason looked up at her, smiling. "Mike's at it again, Mom!"

And he was. The pool was surrounded by fog, by a light, powdery, pink fog that seemed to create a magic realm, beautiful and surreal.

"Oh, no!" she breathed.

And Mike, in cutoffs, bending over the little pellet on the ground that created the fog, laughed.

"Jason," Harry said, "I think that the experiment is over. What say we run over to the main island for an ice cream cone?"

"Mom, Mike, can I?"

Katrina nodded, in a daze. "Yes!"

She thought she saw Harry give Mike a wink, then he and Jason disappeared through the trees.

She wasn't wearing her teal maillot today. She was wearing a two-piece, which was held together by thin spaghetti strings. With her hands on her hips she walked around the pool, ready to lash into her husband. Long before she came to him, she saw that he was grinning. That his silver eyes gleamed like the stars, that he was very lazily stretching out on the sand—waiting for her, expecting her!

"Michael Taylor! You promised—no experiments out of doors!"

He shrugged, patting the clean white expanse of sand beside him. "Come talk to me, I'll try to explain."

"No," she murmured warily, but the magical pink fog was all around her. It made the setting sun even more beautiful; it touched the air with a hint of dampness that made the brush of it against her feel like silk.

She came to him, falling to her knees in the sand. Her hand stretched out, cupping the contours of his cheek. Then she was leaning toward him, desperately hungry for his lips, for the taste of him.

In seconds she was beside him, touching him, stroking him, feeling the ripple of muscle beneath her fingers, luxuriating in the quickening of his breath, and her own. She felt his hands, coursing along her spine, finding strings to pull, then savoring the naked flesh that was revealed. His kisses moved over her breasts until she was on fire, certain that she was the flame that created the glow all around him. She was lost in sensation, swirling on clouds.

The sun streaked over them, crimson, magic, real and unreal. The breeze around them was cool, a shimmering embrace against the rampant heat of their bodies. They were moving in time, in rhythm. The sun made a last, mercurial streak against the sky; it was a pinnacle of beauty and pleasure, a soaring streak of splendor across the sky. And then it began slowly, slowly to ease into shades of softest pink and yellow, drifting, drifting with them as they came, gently and tenderly, back to earth.

Curled against his chest, content and sated, Katrina wrinkled her nose against the damp tendrils of hair on his chest.

"You're definitely a madman, a devil!" she accused him.

"Hmm." He kissed her forehead. "Madly in love with my wife. But"—he moved away from her slightly, meeting her aqua eyes, which were shimmering like the sea—"I've a confession to make. The fog—the pink fog. It wasn't 44DFS. It was just a colored steam pellet."

"Well, my love"—she drew a pattern against his flesh,

following the triangle of hair down his chest, to his waist and below, causing his breath to quicken all over again—"I've a confession too. I knew that it wasn't 44DFS."

"You did?"

"Certainly. You'd never break a promise."

"No, I suppose not."

"And it is our anniversary. And a night out on the town did sound a little tame—for you."

"So you were expecting something." He laughed. "I love to be obliging. . . ."

She smiled and came to his arms again. Night came, and the stars shone down, a gentle, gentle light, made for lovers. The breeze became cooler, and still they lingered, warmed by their love.

At last Mike rose, pulling her to her feet. "We'd better get to the house," he told her. "Jason will be home soon, and Toni is coming in."

"She is?" Katrina gasped with delight.

"I told you I had a baby-sitter for Jason."

"I had thought you meant Harry. But what a nice surprise!"

"I had thought it only fair to tell Toni and Jason together."

"Tell them what?" Katrina demanded, feeling her heart speed.

"About the baby."

Her fingers curled around him, she buried her face against his chest. "I hadn't told you yet!" she whispered. "I meant to tell you tonight. With candlelight and champagne. How did you know?"

He chuckled, smoothing the hair from her face. "One, I'm still a doctor"—he paused to sweep her into his arms—"and two, I am the man who loves you with all his heart, forever."

"Oh, Mike, that's lovely!" she said, wide eyed.

He kissed her nose. "Thank you!"

And laughing together, holding each other, they returned to their house.